Every Block Boy Needs A Little Love 2

TINA J

Disclaimer:

Please be advised that there will be drug use, drinking, discussions regarding incest, and comedy.

Previously...

Arabia

"Hello. Hello." I could barely hear Deray's mom on the phone. There was so much going on inside the hospital, I had to step out.

"Hello." No one answered but she was in the background screaming.

"Hello. Hello." I kept yelling in the phone but she wouldn't answer. Rushing to my car and being careful on the way, I sent Mariah a message letting her know I'm going to see Deray's mom to make sure she was ok. They stayed in Staten Island which wasnt too far from New Jersey.

After the shooting with him, they've been nervous about someone returning to try and get them. Being around my family had me very secure besides the time dumb ass Huff stopped by. In my opinion, the person was there for Deray because I had no beef with anyone and who would follow me.

I pulled out the parking lot and hit the turnpike. It was nerve wrecking that when I tried to call back again, the phone kept going to voicemail. All I could think of was someone may have found and hurt her.

Finally making it to her house, I saw Tricia's car and two other cars in the driveway but no cops. Maybe someone arrived and helped her. Putting my gun inside the back of my pants, I kept my phone on me and stepped out the car. Nothing was out of the ordinary and since it was still daylight, I could see kids playing in their front yards.

It made me wonder if River's son was alright. When the guys told us her son was shot at the playground, we paid for our food and rushed down to the hospital. They may be in a new relationship but all of us knew the two were feeling each other way beforehand. We wanted to be there for her especially after learning some of her past regarding her son. Block found out and told us to let her tell when she was ready.

Slowly walking up the pathway, the door was opened and you could hear voices coming from inside. The screen door happened to be unlocked so I went in and headed straight to the bathroom by the door. I saw his mom standing in the kitchen with his father talking which put my mind at ease for the moment. And besides, it didn't sound like anyone was in danger, and laughter could be heard as I sat on the toilet. My phone vibrated on the counter. I saw it was Mariah and answered.

"Hey, did you get there." I had the phone on my ear while I finished using the bathroom.

"Yea. How is River's son?" I flushed, washed my hands, and checked myself over. Right before she answered, a voice was very familiar outside the door. The person was asking about a ball that used to be in the closet by the front door.

"Hold on, Mariah. I know I'm not bugging."

"Bugging about what?" The second I opened the door, our eyes met.

"Deray."

"Deray?" Mariah questioned on the other end of the phone. I hung up to make sure I'm not dreaming.

"Arabia? When did you get here?" I felt his body to make sure it was real, then smacked fire from his ass.

WHAP!

"What is going on in there?" His parents came in the foyer area where we were.

"When did you find out he was alive?" All of them froze when they saw me.

"Deray, Amani wants you to push her on the swing again." Tricia came from around the corner smiling. She stopped short seeing me.

"All of you fucking knew?"

"Arabia don't get mad at them. I—" He tried to speak but I cut him off. How could he tell me not to be mad when they all knew he didn't die?

"Don't tell me what the fuck to do. Move." I pushed him

out the way and wobbled my pregnant ass to the car. I turned to see all of them standing there.

"Your mothers phone called me and I heard yelling. Thinking she was hurt, I rushed here to help, only to find that my man who I thought was dead, was alive."

"Arabia, aren't you happy?" His mother had the nerve to ask.

"Hell no, I'm not happy that you let me believe your son was dead. You let me believe you were dead. I mourned over you for months. Why, Deray?" I was at the driver's side of my car. There wasn't anything he could say.

"You know what? I don't even care. Stay the fuck away from me. Ahhhh." An excruciating pain shot through my stomach.

"Arabia, what's wrong?" I saw the fear on Deray's face.

"None of your got damn business." Getting in the car, another pain shot through my body. It was like nothing I've ever felt.

"Let me take you to the hospital." He was now on the driver's side trying to keep me from closing the door. I pulled my gun out and pointed it at him.

"Get the fuck away from my car because my shot, is a kill shot and you won't survive." He backed away with his hands up. I hated to be that bitch but fuck him and his family. How dare they not tell me.

Driving to the hospital that the GPS said wasn't far, the pains were coming more and more frequent. I said a prayer to God asking him to save me and my child.

I pulled up close to the door and blew my horn hoping someone would come out. Instead of waiting, I got out and heard tires screeching.

"Move out the wayyyyyy." I heard someone yell as an out of control car hit the curb and hydroplaned in my direction. All I could do was close my eyes and wait for the inevitable to happen.

River

"What's going on, River?" Ryan asked, when I dropped Jasir off. The judge set up a custody hearing for a month away but Ryan let me keep him full time. He got him on the weekends or whenever Jasir called.

"What you mean?"

"Who is this, Jerome, guy, Jasir talking about? I thought we agreed not to let him meet anyone unless we're serious." Over the last three weeks, Block was at the house all the time. He claimed I was his and he was mine, yet we never went anywhere together to show off our relationship.

"I was going to speak with you today about him." He offered me to come in.

"Jasir, let me talk to mommy real quick."

"Ok. Love you, Mommy and tell, Mr. Jerome, I'll be back in two days." He hugged me and put up his two fingers before running off.

"Soooo." I rubbed my hands on top of my jeans.

"His name is Jerome, but he goes by, Block." Ryan began rubbing his temples.

"Please tell me you're not talking about, the guy, Block that everyone scared of." How did he know him? Ryan wasn't a street dude and always stayed away from that area even as a kid.

"I'm not scared of him and you know I'm not in the streets." Ryan put his hands under his chin like he was about to say a prayer.

"I can't tell you who to date but make sure to keep our son safe." He spoke like he had an attitude.

"Ryan." I took offense to him saying that because of the past.

"I'm sorry, River. I wasn't referring to what your mother did. He a street dude was all I meant and dealing with someone like that, you have to be careful." He hugged me and apologized for how he worded it.

"Daddy, when is, Chana coming over? She promised to watch a movie with me." Now it was my turn to question him.

"She's a nurse at the hospital. Her and her pops just moved back from what she said." We both went back and forth about the people we were now dealing with. We did make plans to meet the other person soon.

After saying goodbye, I walked to my van and pulled off. My cell rang when I was halfway home. Seeing it was Block, I smiled before answering.

"Aye! I'm sending you my location. Meet me there in ten minutes." He didn't even let me respond. He disconnected the call and shortly after the location popped up. It was to the same diner me and Jasir saw him at. When I pulled up, he walked out to get me.

"I'm happy as hell you didn't wear your Velma outfit today or those glasses." I pushed him on the arm. I had on some fitted sweats with a V-neck shirt and a pair of Air Max that Block brought me for the security job. He said I had pretty feet and didn't want bad sneakers fucking them up. I wasn't about to complain because Block knew how to suck some toes.

"You still sexy though." He leaned down for a kiss.

"Whatever." He held my hand in his and led the way into the diner. I was surprised to see, Arabia, their mom, Mariah and Onyx, her mom and a few others I didn't know.

"Oh, shit. You must've threw it on my son if he bringing your poor ass out in public." Sticking my tongue at his mom, she flipped me the finger.

For the next few hours we sat in the diner, having a blast. Block's father and other uncle showed up and they started a spades game. It was fun and Mariah seemed to loosen up around me as well.

"Hey, your phone keeps ringing." Arabia passed it to me. I was coming out the bathroom.

"Hey, what's up?" I answered for Ryan. He was so distraught, I couldn't make out a word he was saying. Block took the phone.

"Wait! What?" Block's entire family began staring at me because panic struck instantly trying to understand him.

"Ok, where are you?" Not sure what he said but the look on

Block's face said something was terribly wrong. Once he hung up, he made his way to where the guys were. All of them turned in my direction.

"What's wrong? What happened?" I questioned but he wouldn't answer.

"Let's go." Without another word, Block lifted me up.

"Did something happen to my son? What's going on?" My vision was becoming blurry from me about to cry, one of the contacts fell out and now I really couldn't see out that eye. Block saw it, placed me in his truck, went to my van and returned with my purse and glasses. I brought them wherever I went just in case the contacts irritated me. I've worn them a lot more since the gender reveal and now that my eye doctor gave me a new prescription for it, my Medicaid covered it.

"Block, please tell me what's wrong." Focused on the road, he had me scared by how fast he was going.

"Block, please."

"Your son was at the park with his father and something happened." My heart started racing faster. As soon as I went to ask another question, we were pulling up at the emergency room. I didn't wait for him to park and rushed inside.

"Ryan! Ryan! Where is my son? What happened?" There was a woman standing next to him. She must be the chick he was seeing.

"I don't know, River. We were at the park and outta nowhere there was a drive by. Him and two other kids were hit. River there was so much blood. I don't know what I'll do if he doesn't make it." My life flashed before my eyes when he said my son was shot and the amount of blood he saw.

"No. No, no, no. Don't tell me someone shot my son. Don't you tell me that. Ryan, say you're lying." I started punching him in the chest. He tried grabbing my hands.

"River, I jumped on top of him but it was too late." Tears were streaming down his face and the chick was crying as well.

"I got her." Block picked me up.

"River, you gotta relax. He's gonna be ok." My body was shaking so bad, I started hyperventilating. My lips were trembling and my glasses kept sliding down.

"Block, my son. Oh, God. Please don't let him die. I need to get in the back to see him. He's gonna want his mother." I did everything possible to break free but he wasn't letting me go.

"What the fuck?" Ryan barked. I turned to see him staring at the last person who needed to be here.

"Where is he?" When she went to the nurses station to ask questions, I couldn't believe my eyes.

"Who the fuck are you?" Block shouted and I couldn't answer him. Why was she here? Who told her what happened?

"I'm River's mother and that was my grandson who was shot." I couldn't believe she was in my presence. But what really took the cake was Ryan's friend knowing who she was.

"Louise?"

"Who the fuck are you?" My mother snapped.

"I'm your daughter." I could see my mother's face. It wasn't scared or mad but more or less nervous about what this chick would say.

"Do you have a sister?" Block asked and Ryan stared at me too.

"Not that I know of." I asked him to walk with me closer so I could hear clearer. The chick moved in close as well to finish what she needed to say.

"Get the fuck away from me." My mother was adamant about not hearing anything else.

"Oh, you don't remember the daughter you gave away." I gasped at the woman's revelation.

"The family of Jasir Rogers." A doctor came out from the other side.

"Yes. I'm his mother and he's his father." Block started to walk away but I grabbed his hand. He probably didn't think I wanted him to stay but that was far from the truth.

"I need you." He nodded and wrapped his arms around my waist.

"Let's go in another room. There's a lot going on out here." I noticed Block's family walking in.

"Charlene?" The chick knew Onyx's grandmother too. I'm not even sure why she came here.

"Why you here?" Block asked her on the way in the room.

"My great nephew was shot." It was like a nightmare that I couldn't wake up from. This chick continued unleashing bombs.

"Go inside, River. I'll be in shortly." Block attempted to push me inside but I froze when the chick said her last statement.

"So, you're Charlene. The bitch who forced my mother and father to have sex, knowing they were siblings."

"River, it's Jasir." Ryan ran out the room crying harder.

"What? What did the doctor say?"

"He said—" Before he could relay what the doctor said, I heard what sounded like a gun.

CLICK!

"Bitch, I've been looking for you."

CHAPTER 1

River

AT THE HOSPITAL...

Ith was complete silence in the waiting room once that man pulled a gun on Charlene. He could pass for his early forties, salt and pepper hair, short beard and, was in decent shape from the look of his muscles coming out the T-shirt. He had on some white Air Force one sneakers and the evil expression on his face scared me.

"Who the fuck are you?" Onyx had his gun on the guy, and now Block did too. I still had no idea what was going on.

"Take her to speak with the doctor." Block told Ryan, who had to basically pick me up. I was frozen stiff in the spot because I've never been around anyone with a gun.

"Block, are you coming?" I wanted him to be my support system but then again, the chick who came with Ryan was standing out there next to the guy.

"I'll be there shortly." He spoke without turning around. When we stepped inside the room, the doctor was standing there terrified. The entire scene was very chaotic to say the least. I'm surprised the cops weren't here yet.

"Are you ok?" The doctor asked, making me take a seat.

"I'm fine."

"You sure, River. You're shaking and blood is coming out your nose." Ryan handed me some tissues off the table in here.

"Did you get hit?" He grabbed the stethoscope from around his neck, placed it on my chest and put his two fingers on my wrist.

"No." He listened for a few seconds and spoke to Ryan.

"Sir, get me a nurse in here and tell them I need a stretcher." He yelled.

"I'm ok, doctor. Just tell me about my son." Nothing mattered to me but Jasir. I haven't been able to find out anything due to the chaos outside.

"Ma'am, your pressure is 180/101. You're not ok." He stood up and I grabbed his wrists tight.

"Please tell me if I'm son is ok."

"What the fuck going on?" Block barked, running in behind the two people with a stretcher.

"I'm ok, Block." He made his way over to me and stared for a second.

"What's wrong with her?" How could he tell something was wrong?

"I don't care what's wrong with me. Is my son going to be ok?" One of the nurses had me stand in order to get on the stretcher. Before anyone answered me, my eyes started to flutter and the room started spinning.

"Get her in a room, NOW! Her pressure is too high. She's going into cardiac arrest." The doctor shouted and the stretcher began to move.

"What?" I could hear Block yelling but no words would come out.

"Take care of her." Were the last words I heard him say.

* * *

BEEP! BEEP! I heard opening my eyes. Staring at the ceiling for a few seconds, I remembered what happened and tried to jump up. I felt a pull and looked down at the IV that was taped down to my arm with a bandage wrapped around it. I felt monitors all over my chest and the cuff around my bicep began to tighten up.

"River, calm down." Looking at Block staring, made me uncomfortable. He was dressed differently from what I remember and to be honest, he looked good as hell.

"How's my son? Did he make it? What floor did they put him on?" I started peeling the wires to the heart monitor off. Block sat down next to me on the bed.

"He's fine, River."

"I need to see him with my own eyes." Still trying to get up, a nurse walked in smiling.

"Are you ok?"

"She just woke up. Can you fix the monitor?" He answered for me.

"Block, I need to see—" He shushed me with a kiss.

"When the nurse finishes, we'll discuss that. Right now, let her work." He was very calm and his voice was soothing. Lying back on the bed, I waited for the nurse to fix the monitor and asked if she could get me a water basin to at least brush my teeth and wash my face.

After handling my hygiene in the bed, it dawned on me that something was in between my legs. Removing the cover, I gasped at the sight of a catheter. It had some urine in it which made me gag. Block covered it up and sat next to me.

"Here." He passed me his phone and I let the tears drop.

Jasir had on a hospital gown with a white bracelet on his arm. Ryan sat on the side of his bed coloring with him. Ms. Rogers was on the other side drinking what appeared to be a coffee.

"Jasir, can you tell, Mommy, you're ok?" I heard Block's voice in the background of the video.

"I'm ok, Mommy. Look, I got shot with a gun." He showed the cast on his leg and another one on from his wrist to his elbow. There was also a big white bandage around his head. I hated this for him.

"When are you gonna wake up? Daddy, said we can go home when you open your eyes, and Mr. Jerome coming over to play the game again." He smiled, looking into the camera.

"Thanks, Lil Man. Your mom will be happy to see this."

Jasir blew a kiss at the phone and went back to coloring with his dad. I handed the phone over to Block.

"One bullet hit him in the leg, another in his forearm, and he hit his head from the fall. There's no bleeding on the brain or any other complications. He's gonna be alright, River." I cried harder hearing my son was ok.

"This was the second time he almost lost his life to the stupidity of someone else." He held my hand in his.

"What happened the first time?" He wiped my eyes and listened to me tell the story for what I'm hoping will be the last time.

"Ma, I'm going to work. Jasir is in his room watching television." I kept the door opened to her room whenever I went to work. It was the only time she kept an eye on him.

I worked at the mall part time to have extra money to take care of my son. Ryan was working as well but he just started at the hospital with his mom. He gave me money whenever he got paid, but what about the week when he didn't have money and Jasir needed diapers or food.

Anyway, I kissed my son goodbye, and made sure his television was on cartoons. He had his snacks and my mother's room was directly next door. If Jasir roamed out the bedroom she would see him.

I really didn't want to leave him with her because my whole life, she never left the room. However, I only worked four hours a day so it should've been fine.

Locking the front door, I ran to the bus stop in just enough time to make the bus. I had to be at work by one and it was twelve.

It was pay day too, so when I got off, me and Jasir were going to the store.

Long story short, I came home and called out to Jasir. When he didn't answer, I went to the bedroom assuming he was taking a nap. He wasn't in there so I checked my mother's room and no Jasir.

"Where is Jasir?" My mother ignored me and continued watching television. Our house wasn't big which meant he could only be in the bathroom or hiding.

"Oh my, God!" I found my son on the bathroom floor foaming at the mouth. His eyes were rolling and his body shook. Falling to my knees, I noticed pill bottles opened on the floor. How the hell did he even get these? They were my mother's medication for her bi-polar, and another one for depression. The pills were spread out on the floor which meant he possibly could've ingested both, but how many. Sticking my fingers down his throat, he vomited a little and took a deep breath. Still his body was weak and I could tell he could barely catch his breath.

"Jasir, baby. Wake up." Patting his face trying to get him up, nothing was happening.

"Maaaaaa, call an ambulance." No response.

"Oh, God. Please wake up." Lifting him off the ground, I ran to my mother's room, laid him on his side, grabbed her cell and called 911. My mother sat up staring at Jasir convulsing.

"Get off my phone." She tried to take it from me as I read the address off to the dispatcher.

"Please, hurry."

"Ma'am. The cops are coming..." Before I could say anything

else, she ripped the phone from my hands. At the moment, I couldn't focus on what she was doing. Running to the front door with Jasir in my hands, I opened it to wait. Praying they would get here in time.

Exactly two minutes later, paramedics ran in. They rushed out with him and said to meet them at the hospital because there was no time to wait for me. Little did I know, the cops told them to leave me.

"Ma'am, what happened here?" Two cops started asking me questions about what took place. A half hour later, a woman stepped in and I knew then, my son was going to be removed from me. She resembled the same woman who had been here countless times trying to take me, only she was younger.

"River, your son will be placed in foster care due to neglect."

"What? Please don't take my son. He's all I got." The woman kept a straight face. I begged her for twenty minutes but to no avail did it work. She packed my son clothes and a few toys and headed to the door.

"Don't take my son!" I screamed. A woman cop tried to calm me down. I punched her in the face a few times.

"Please take him to his father." I yelled to the woman as I was being arrested. I looked at my house and Louise Thomas stood at the door smoking a cigarette as if nothing happened.

"It's ok." Block wrapped his arms around me as I told him the truth.

"She tried to kill my son." I finally admitted something I stayed in denial about.

"Why?"

"I never knew why my mother hated me. She always said I was an abomination and any kids I had would be too."

"Do you know why she said that?" I wiped my eyes on his shirt.

"No. I don't even know why she was here. Block, please make sure security knows not to allow her in to see him." He lifted my head.

"No one can get on the floor with him unless I know who it is. I'm cool with the charge nurse."

"Great. One of your many freaks." I joked to get out of a somber mood.

"Actually, I've never slept with her. She tried, but I couldn't get past her face." He shrugged.

"Huh?"

"She had a beautiful spirit but that big mole on the side of her face, made me nauseous." I shook my head.

"You're a mess." He rested his back against the bed. We laid there in silence for a few minutes.

"How you get pregnant and lose the baby right away?" *Did he just say I was pregnant?*

"Say what?" I looked up at him.

"You must've gotten pregnant the first time we had sex because that's how far along the doctor said you were. The stress and you going into cardiac arrest caused a miscarriage." My hands immediately went to my stomach, then the catheter. It's when I noticed the blood inside it.

"That's crazy. We used condoms the second time."

"Didn't I say it happened after the first time. For someone

who supposed to smart as Velma, you're not being smart now." I popped him on the arm.

"It's cool though. We barely knew one another and bringing a baby into the equation, would've complicated things."

"How?"

"What you mean how? What if I don't want you no more? That pussy A1 but you might get lazy in the bed now that I said it was good." Instead of engaging with his ignorance, I closed my eyes.

"If it's meant for us to procreate again, we will but I'm telling you right now, my kid getting corrective surgery on his or her eyes right away. They will not have fishbowl glasses as kids."

"I can't stand you and Jasir don't wear glasses."

"True. He must have his dad's vision." Block said anything whether it made sense or not.

For the rest of the night, he stayed with me. The doctor came in explaining how I was down for three days which was the reason for the bag. He put me on two medications, one for my pressure and another for my heart. Evidently, he found an extra heartbeat or something. I wasn't paying attention once he mentioned me going home. Jasir was being released in the morning too. Today was a good day.

"Get out." I didn't have to turn around to know Deray was in my home; I could smell his cologne. It was my favorite and he wore it whenever I came over or we went out.

It's been four days since I found out he was alive. Sadly, the surprise sent me to the hospital where I almost lost the baby. To make matters worse, a car skidded in my direction. A tech happened to be coming outside and moved me out the way fast enough. The car did go through one of the windows and the person had to be rushed inside.

Anyway, the doctor checked me over and at six months, the baby was doing fine. He said I may have pulled a muscle or moved wrong which caused the pain. He allowed me to listen to my son's heartbeat and see him on the screen for reassurance. Now I'm in my bed minding my own business and here he was.

"I'm sorry, Arabia." I chuckled at his ignorance. Forcefully removing the covers from my legs, I scooted off the bed.

"Sorry? Sorry for what? Huh?" No response. Grabbing my robe off the door, I put it on and went downstairs to get a bottle of water. Turning around, he stood there against the wall staring at me.

"What part of get out don't you get." Swallowing almost the whole bottle, I waited for a response that I'm not sure I wanted to hear. What could he possibly say that would make me understand why he faked his death?

"Can I explain?"

"Explain what? How you let me believe you died? What type of fucking game was that?" I slammed the bottle on the counter.

"Arabia." He reached out for me when I walked past him.

"Then, your family went along with the lie." I turned to him.

"You were spending time with your daughter while I was attending prenatal appointments alone." That shit hurt me to my soul to know he spent time with one kid and not the other.

"You weren't alone, Arabia. I was on the phone." The look on my face was pure disgust.

"Wait a minute."

"I had Tricia keep me on the phone. When the doctor showed you our son, she had me on FaceTime." I know that bitch didn't go along with him, then again she was at the house too.

"WHAT?"

11

"You didn't know because she had an earpiece on."

"Oh, all you people are grimy." I wasn't holding my feelings back at all.

"The reason they were gone when you left the appointment was because I was in the car. I wanted to come in but they advised me not to." I shook my head listening to him explain. Why did he listen to them? Was it because they didn't want him around me?

"I've watched over you every night on the camera. I saw that nigga put his hands on you and I saw you crying." He had access to the cameras inside my home. It never dawned on me that he could be watching. I guess it wouldn't since he was supposed to be dead.

"You saw me crying and never said a word. You saw him hit me and did nothing? What kind of man are you?" I sat on my couch staring at him trying to come up with something else.

"I understand why you're upset."

"Upset. Nah, nigga. I'm fucking pissed and nobody will take that away from me."

"Arabia." He tried to sit by me and I immediately moved.

"This shit happened over you." He lifted his shirt and showed me the scars from the shooting.

"The shooting was my fault?" He came to me.

"Yo, nigga did this." Not trying to hear anything he had to say, I walked to the front door.

"That night I went to open the door, your punk ass nigga was standing there with a few of his boys. He told the nigga to shoot me for fucking his girl. I saw him run afterwards like the bitch he was."

"Wait a minute. How did Huff know who you were or where you lived?" I never assumed he would follow me because he was always out with some chicks.

"He had been following you from what he said. He told those niggas to run up in my house to find and kill you. Why you think I got shot in two other places?" He showed me a scar on his arm and his leg. I didn't want to hear anymore.

"Even after being shot in the stomach, I tried to keep them from coming in. Those extra set of shots put me down and I'm so fucking sorry for not telling you I was alive. I couldn't take the chance of him sending someone to finish the job." His hands were on the side of my face. He swiped his thumbs under my eye to wipe away the tears.

"There were so many times, I wanted to come for you but it was never the right time." He gently kissed my lips. As much as I knew this wasn't the right thing to do, I couldn't stop it.

"I'm sorry, Arabia." He removed my robe and led me upstairs into the bedroom.

"You have no idea how much I've missed being inside you." Wasting no time, he laid me on the bed, removed all his clothes and inserted himself slow.

"Fuck, I'm about to cum." He moaned and a minute later, he did. Deray didn't lay there like most men would. No, he got on his knees, scooted me to the edge of the bed and devoured my pussy. My body shook each time he extracted an orgasm from me. Once he entered again, Deray made love to me off and on for as long as my body could take it.

I laid in the bed staring down at him sleeping, I ran my fingers over the wounds. The stomach one was extremely deep with a scar leading up to his chest. The one on his arm was the size of a quarter and the one on his leg, was rather big but not like the one on his stomach. I was happy he didn't die but still fucked up about how him and his family handled it, and for that he had to go.

"Deray." He stirred in his sleep but pulled me closer.

"Deray." I nudged him a tad bit harder.

"You ok?" He was very disoriented.

"I'm fine but you gotta go." I sat up and noticed his confusion. Without saying a word, he got dressed.

"Arabia." I put my hand up to keep him from speaking and walked downstairs. As much as I desperately wanted him to stay, it wasn't a good idea. He'll think what he did was ok and it's never ok to fool anyone with a death.

Going down the stairs, I started crying because I was in love with him and the fact he tricked me didn't sit right in my spirit. It made me uneasy about him being here. What if he pretended to die again? Would I be able to take it?

"I love you with all my heart, Deray." I told him when he stood in front of me.

"I'm in love with you too but I understand." He opened the front door.

"Just know I did it for both of our safety and when I find him, he will take his last breath."

14

"Find him? He hasn't been hiding." To my knowledge, Huff been out and about even after Block whooped his ass.

"It's clear you have no idea what's going on. Maybe you should speak with your brother."

"You trying to say he knew you were alive?" I folded my arms across my chest.

"Your brother would've told you, Arabia." I had to agree. Block saw how distraught his death had me and would've never kept that information from me.

"Just go."

"If you need me, I'm a phone call away." That shit aggravated me to hear him say.

"Clearly, you've been a phone call away but you and your family pretended you were heavens away." I opened the door for him.

"You know what's crazy, Tricia said, everything wasn't what it seemed at the repast. Your mom said, he's always with you at the doctor's appointment." I shook my head.

"They were giving me clues but I was so messed up about losing you, I didn't see them." How could I miss those signs?

"My mother said something wasn't right when we left the hospital the night you were shot. I mean, why wouldn't they let me see you." He stood there letting me vent.

"I'll tell you why; it's because you were still alive." I started punching him in the chest and crying.

"I didn't deserve that, Deray. How could you do that to me? I hate you." He pulled me in for a hug and held me tight.

"Just go." I pushed myself off him.

"I fucked up, Arabia and I'm sorry for everything but I'm gonna keep coming around until you forgive me." That made me laugh. He stepped on the porch and turned around.

"I could never forgive a dead man walking." I slammed the door in his face.

"What about my son?" He yelled on the other side.

"He won't know about you. Continue to play dead." Walking away from the door, I heard a loud noise. When I turned around, Deray stood there breathing heavy. He had kicked my door off the hinges.

"Stay mad at me forever but I will see my son. Are we clear?" He now stood in front of me breathing like the Incredible Hulk.

"Deray, get out."

"Are we fucking clear about my son?" I nodded with my back against the wall.

"If you don't wanna be with me, a'ight cool. But when you speak on not letting me be in my son's life that's where we have a problem." I've never seen him this angry and it scared me.

"I'll be at the next appointment." He backed up from me.

"If you even think about entertaining another nigga, I'll fucking kill you." And just like that, he was gone.

Did he really threaten me? How dare he tell me not to be with someone else? Plopping down on the couch, I held my head in my hands and cried. I cried for him not being dead, cried that he was here and made love to me, and cried that we would never be the same after this.

* * *

"Damn, he kicked the door down and the frame came off. What you do?" Mariah joked about the front door.

Last night after Deray left and once I got myself together, I stayed with my parents. It wasn't possible for me to stay here without a door. All my mother kept saying was, *"I knew it. His family was too calm leaving the hospital."*

"I kicked him out and said my son won't know him, and he could continue playing dead." I shrugged and saw the guys I hired to fix the door pulling up.

"Arabia."

"I know, Mariah. It was messed up but what else could I say. One minute he's dead, and the next he was alive. Who does that to the person they love?" I started crying again.

"Look, Arabia. I would be doing the same thing to, Onyx had he done me that way. But the fact remains that he is alive." I nodded with a smile.

"He looked so handsome last night."

"I know y'all had sex too, didn't you." I laughed.

"If you don't want to forgive him, I understand but don't keep his baby away. Matter of fact, does Huff know you're expecting?"

"No." I hadn't been outside and when he did stop by that last time, my stomach wasn't big.

"Do you think he'll assume the baby is his?" That was a question Huff shouldn't even ask.

"He shouldn't when we haven't had sex long before this pregnancy." I rubbed my stomach after feeling my son kick.

"It's going to be a problem when he does so be careful." Who was I fooling? Mariah was absolutely correct, especially when Huff asked me on a few occasions to have a child by him. Thankfully, we didn't have kids because it would've been harder to keep him away.

Deray had to be hurt hearing me say to stay dead but what did he expect. You can't tell people you're dead, have a service and actually stay gone. Had I not stopped by, I'm not even sure when he planned on telling me that he was alive.

"You're gonna be fine, Arabia." Mariah hugged me.

"I hope so." Was the only response that seemed appropriate to say.

CHAPTER 3

Onyx

"Ernie? What are you doing here?" My grandmother called out with her hands in the air. I had no idea who this man was and even though she was a bitch, he had no right pulling a gun on her.

"That's right, bitch. I've been waiting years to find you, and make you pay for your sins." Was he into church or some shit. I looked at Block who had his weapon pulled as well and pointed at him. He shrugged.

"Ernie." Now River's mother spoke to the same man. For some reason my mother was in complete shock.

"I don't give a fuck who you are. Take that gun off my grandmother."

"Your grandmother? Bitch, you had kids. Were you doing the same thing to them? You bitch." This nigga pistol whipped the hell outta my grandmother.

"Oh shit." Block said what I wanted to but couldn't. The guy *started kicking her in the back and anywhere else his foot connected. Everyone stared at me, and for the moment his pain showed. Whatever my grandmother did, he was releasing his anger.*

"Ok. Ok. That's enough." I grabbed him by the shirt and tossed him against the wall. He was a big dude too.

"Is she dead?" Some chick asked, standing over top of her. Someone pulled her away.

"Who the fuck are you?"

"Let's go, Chana. We'll catch River later." She walked over to him.

"Hold the fuck up. You ain't catching shit later." Block made that very clear.

"I don't know who you are but that's my motherfucking daughter so yes, I will catch her later." He said in a matter of fact tone.

"Nigga, what?" Block hit that nigga hard as fuck. When he stumbled back, all of us stopped Block from continuing.

"Bro, if that's really her pops, River won't be happy." My words were able to calm him. He snatched away from everyone and went to check on her.

"Somebody better tell me right now what the fuck is going on." I snapped, staring at my mother who was shaking her head. River's mother walked past me with her head down and Charlene appeared to be dead on the floor.

"Babe, you ok?" Mariah was standing at the door staring at me.

"I'm good." She must've caught me reminiscing about what took place at the hospital a few days ago.

"You sure?" She questioned, coming toward me.

"Positive. How's Arabia?" She wanted Mariah to come over to talk.

I had her sit on my lap. Rubbing her belly always put me in a different mind space no matter what I had going on. Mariah rested her head on my shoulder.

"Babe, do me a favor. If you ever die and have to fake your death, please tell me." I had her look at me.

"What you talking about?"

"Deray is alive." I was shocked in a way but not too much. When he died and his family remained calm and wouldn't let Arabia see him, left questions in my head too. Why couldn't she see him? Now we know why; the nigga wasn't dead.

"Get the fuck outta here." She proceeded to tell me everything Arabia told her.

"I understand why he did it and I probably would've done the same." She gave me a dirty look.

"However, I'm not gonna keep it from the woman I'm in love with, regardless if it was her man who did it."

"He did threaten her about being with another man." She laughed.

"Word?" I chuckled because most men do the same thing when they're wrong.

"How dare him? Like, he really disappeared for a few months and expected her to welcome him with open arms."

"I bet they slept together tho, didn't they?" I busted out laughing when she said yes.

Arabia was in love with him and no matter how mad she was, she made sure to give him something to remember her by while she made him suffer.

Anybody who listened to Mariah tell that story knows Arabia ain't going nowhere. She was about to make him work to earn her trust and love, and that's how it should be. Granted, I would've stayed at the house anyway but we all do things differently.

* * *

"Hey, Honey. What's going on?" My mother walked out the kitchen to greet me. I had just come from visiting Arabia with Block to find out what really happened to Deray and why he did it. Mariah told me but it made sense to hear it from her as well in case my wife left something out.

"When are you gonna tell me what that was about at the hospital?" She blew over the cup to cool off the coffee.

"Sit." She patted the seat next to her.

"I'm only able to tell you what I know. Everything else would have to come from my mother or her siblings." I nodded.

"First off, I learned about Ernie and Louise when you did." I believed that. Especially since I've never had an aunt or uncle from her side of the family.

"Say what?"

"To my knowledge, Charlene was an only child. I never met her parents and was told they perished in a fire." She took a sip of the coffee and sat the cup down.

"Throughout my high school years, people used to say, Charlene was a Cougar and wanted the younger kids." I sucked my teeth.

"Exactly. Anyway, she would attend the football and basketball games as well as the track meets, even though I wasn't on any of those teams, nor did I cheerlead." My mother hated sports and felt like the cheerleaders were whores who fucked all the players. Her words, not mine. If you asked me, I enjoyed fucking all those cheerleaders during my high school years.

"A few times, some of the younger boys would come over at night pretending to be there for me. Now you know at this time, I already had you so I wasn't thinking about any of them." I sat there listening.

"She got arrested when you were three for having sex with the kids from school." I turned my nose up.

"I'm not excusing what she did but remember, your grand-mother was barely thirty and they were all eighteen years of age." She did have my mother at a young age and unfortunately, the cycle continued with my mother. I'm going to do every-thing in my power for it to stop there and not have my daughter in the same situation at that age.

"Still, that's nasty as fuck."

"Right. However, she got off and was cleared of any wrong-doing because she was no authority to them and legally, they were of age to consent." I couldn't believe the things my mother was saying.

"Long story short, some of the moms whooped her ass for sleeping with their sons. Yet, it didn't stop her and only ignited the fire for her to sleep with them again. I mean, they were staying the night with her. Can you imagine being a sixteen year old hearing those boys and your grandmother moaning in the other room." She shook her head in disgust.

"Nah, and I don't want to."

"Lo and behold, your stupid ass father got ahold of the information and one night when he was at the house, he crept out the room when me and you were asleep. You woke up for some juice and I heard her calling his name. The bitch even had the door cracked." I knew she left my father at a young age but until this day, I never knew why.

"Here I was pregnant with my second child and my mother was sleeping with my boyfriend."

"Wait a minute."

"No, he had just turned eighteen the week before." He was a few years older than my mother.

"One thing I can say about her was when it came to outsiders, she refused to sleep with anyone under the age of eighteen. She had to see their ID's first." To me that still didn't make it right.

"So you're telling me, she was basically a pimp."

"If that's what you wanna call her." She took another sip of her drink.

"Because I thought my grandparents were dead and she had

no siblings, I had to stay put until I could afford to move out. Lucky for me, at the time I turned eighteen, an apartment became available through housing. Since your father felt bad about sleeping with your grandmother, he begged his mother who ran housing at the time to give me a place." Crazy how we lived there until Montell found me. Even my dad's brothers called my father a fucked up individual for sleeping with Charlene from what she said. My mother chalked it up to him being young and immature.

"When that other shit happened, I felt like a failure because how could I not see that coming." She spoke of the family shit that I hated to think about.

"My heart was broken so bad and... and... no one deserved to ever go through that." Tears started to stream down her face.

"Ma, all you gotta do is say the word. It's all I've been waiting for." She wiped her face.

"Is it sad to say, I can't. Charlene is still my mother." I understood even though I didn't want to.

"Come here." I made her stand to hug her.

"What happened was not your fault and no one blamed you, not even Raymond."

"I wanna believe that but he gives me a look that makes me think he hated me." I tried to comfort my mother but right now she was hysterical. I yelled out to my stepfather to come get her. They were married at a courthouse two years ago. She didn't want a big wedding if all her family couldn't attend.

"Hey, what's wrong? Is she ok?" He took my mom's hand and pulled her into him.

"I'll let her tell you. Meanwhile, keep an eye on her. The last time she was this upset, we had to get her from the hospital." He promised not to leave my mother side.

When my mother thinks about her past and Raymond, she falls into a state of depression. What happened was not her fault and honestly, I'm surprised she didn't beg me to kill Charlene. Then again, it was her mother and I'm sure the choice wasn't an easy one.

I hopped in my car and took the two hour ride to go visit Raymond. It's been a couple of weeks since the last time we saw one another and we needed to have a talk anyway.

CHAPTER 4

Block

"Where you been?" I cringed hearing this bitch behind me. Turning around in the store, Dana stood there wearing a fitted maxi dress with some opened toe sandals. It was almost summer so the outfit was cute but the snarl on her face made everything about her ugly.

"What you want?" I picked up candy and some Tylenol for Jasir.

I've been over there every day since he came home. His father has as well, and even stayed the night. They didn't want to keep bringing him back and forth with the two casts on. I didn't have a problem with it as long as I'm there too. I'm cool with their friendship but it doesn't change the fact that they fucked in the past; a lot at that.

When she mentioned they were each other's first, it aggravated me even more. It made me wonder if she had done the same things to him, she did to me. If he was hooked on her pussy the way I was? I know they haven't slept together in years but it don't stop a nigga from reminiscing; especially if it was good.

"Can I see you tonight?" She ran her fingers down my arm. I swatted her hand away.

"Bitch, are you crazy? What if someone thought you were my girl?" Glancing around the store to see if anyone was looking, I noticed some older folks not paying us any mind.

"What's wrong with that?" She felt offended. Blowing my breath, I had to break it to her gently. River asked me to try and be more sensitive when speaking to women.

"Look, I have someone."

"It better not be that bitch, I helped get the apartment." See, I tried to be gentle and look where it got me. It really irked me when women called another woman a bitch and didn't know her. I pushed her stupid ass up against the can foods.

"Owwww." A can of spaghetti fell on top of her.

"You told me, she was your cousin." She rubbed her head.

"It don't matter what I said. You wanted the dick in exchange for the deal. It was an even switch so we done." I went to leave and stopped when she started talking shit.

"Well, you better tell her, my sister, yea she was the social worker who took her son before." I swung my body around. Dana had a smug look on her face and it pissed me off.

"Yup, she was assigned the case again." Why would child services get involved and I knew her sister too. We had sex a few times, I wonder if she knew.

"She wasn't even there when her son got hurt. And it was an accident, even made the news." The shooting was on the news for three days due to kids getting injured.

I left her standing there and went to put the few items on the counter. Just my luck it was the same ratchet cashier from before. Her facial expression made me laugh because she probably thought I was gonna say something smart.

"Doesn't matter." This bitch didn't know when to stop.

"This was the second time her son got hurt. The system don't care how it happened." She shrugged and attempted to walk away. I yoked her up by the back of her dress as the cashier rang my stuff up.

"Since you tryna be smart, let me hurt your feelings real quick." She rolled her eyes. The girl gave me the total and I gave her my card.

"I fucked your sister a few times, matter of fact right after you one time because your pussy was so dry, I had to find someone wetter to make it feel better."

"Oh shit." The cashier handed me the card. I let go of her dress.

"You're lying." I pulled my phone out and read off her sisters number.

"Clara was her name and if I had to choose whose pussy was better, I'd go with her and you know why." Embarrassment was written all over Dana's face, especially since the cashier was all in our conversation.

"She begged for the dick as much as you but she knew her

place; you don't. Thanks." I grabbed the stuff and walked to the door.

"You think fucking a nigga for favors gives you a right to try and blackmail him."

"That wasn't—"

"Shut the fuck up!" I barked walking out the door and to my car. Like the desperate bitch she was, she followed.

"You thought saying some shit about my girl son would make me weak. You thought oh, he'd fuck me to save her kid. Am I right?" She said nothing.

"Let me tell you the type of nigga, I am since you clearly don't know." I stood very close to her. Dana was a pretty woman and her pussy was ok except that time she was dry as hell. She was about to learn that I'm not that nigga she can play games with.

"If at any chance your sister or any child service worker goes to her house, I'll assume you sent them there and then, I'm coming for you." She backed up when she noticed I was serious.

"Once I'm done with you, I'll go down your family tree and start taking lives until I feel better." She started shaking when I placed her hand on my gun that was in my waist.

"Don't fuck with me, Dana because you won't win."

"I'm sorry. It's just—"

"It's just nothing. Get the fuck out my face." I mushed her and laughed as she fell in one of those bushes they have in front of the parking spaces.

"Oh, tell your sister, I might be by to fuck later." I hit her with the peace sign, hopped in my ride and left. I'm not sleeping with her or her sister anymore. It felt good watching Dana tear up. I bet her ass learn the next time.

* * *

"Babe, this feels good." I had River facing against the wall with her legs spread open. Her pussy was inhaling my dick just the way I wanted. Each time I bent my knees and came back up, her body would shake.

"How good?" I pulled her away just a little to put her body in an arch. I spread her ass cheeks open enough to stick my finger in her ass and River lost control of her body. She came extremely hard and I enjoyed watching. Pulling out, I laid her on the bed and stared down at how beautiful she was.

"I'm tryna be in this all night." I slid in and River held her legs wide for me. My dick disappeared over and over inside.

"Fuck me harder." She moaned.

"Your son's father in the other room." She had the music up but I'm sure he could hear. I didn't really care; it was more of me tryna be respectful to Jasir. It's not my fault she wanted to fuck while he was here.

"Soooo. Fuckkk yessss. Don't stop baby." I continued going harder and harder. The headboard was banging against the wall.

"Shit." I moaned. The feeling of how wet she was and her pussy constricting was driving me crazy.

"Let me try something." She stopped, had me sit with my back against the headboard and stood over me.

"You rode me plenty of times, Ma." My hands roamed her legs.

"Not like this." When she dropped hard and got up to do it again, it was my turn to lose control. She wasn't doing the normal riding on her knees or her feet. She'd stand up and drop hard as fuck, and that had me losing it. My dick felt like she was teasing me by dropping her pussy on me and taking it away. I can't explain it.

"Fuck, River." She did it again but spread her legs wide like she was in a split. With her tiny frame it wasn't hard for her to be flexible. She started going in circles in that position and I swear she strung me out. Her pussy was wide open and my dick was inside deep.

"Block, I don't know what you're doing to me. But you better not ever give this dick awayyyyyyy. Yesssssss, baby. Yessssss." She remained in that split like position and threw her tongue in my mouth. My hands were squeezing her ass as she went in circles.

"Cum for me, Jerome Winston." She shocked me by saying my government. I know she knew it but she's never called me anything but Block.

"You better hold on." Her arms went around my neck, I put both of her legs in the crook of my arms and fucked the shit outta her from the bottom.

"Baby, I'm cummingggggg." She sang as my dick twitched and released everything I had. It felt like my ass couldn't stop.

"Don't move, River." She chuckled as she hid her face in my neck.

"I'm not ever leaving you." She whispered and rested her head on my shoulder.

"I'll blow your got damn brains out if you even think about another nigga." I jerked her head back by the hair. River had me so gone, I was ready to kill her or any nigga who looked at her.

"Block."

"I mean it; take me for a joke if you want." I kissed her collarbone and let my fingers slide up and down her spine.

"You're my first boyfriend, Block. I'm not sure how to treat you or what it's like to be the main woman in a man's life. I do know cheating won't be tolerated, neither will putting your hands on me, or verbally abusing me."

"Never." She kissed my lips a few times.

"I'm finally happy, my son is ok and you're in my life. I'll never hurt you and I expect the same."

"I got you and Jasir, River. Shit, my family wanted me and you together anyway, and you were already pregnant by me. We can't get no tighter than this." She smiled and slowly lifted herself off. Her juices slid out onto my stomach but nothing prepared me for something I don't think she wanted me to see.

"River." She turned around to tie the belt on her robe she put on.

"Come here." Sashaying her sexy ass to me, she bumped into the dresser. Shorty really had a hard time seeing without her glasses. I watched her put them on and moved to the edge of the bed.

"Turn around."

"What happened? Did my period come? Is it blood?" She was focused on the wrong thing. Lifting the back of her robe just above her ass, I let a grin creep on my face.

"Why did you get this?" She started blushing. It was a small tattoo that read, *"Block's Lady"* on her side. It wasn't big and you had to be looking to see it.

"I told you, I never had a man. Isn't this what chicks are supposed to do to show the man they love him." Her words caught me off guard like a motherfucker.

"You're in love with me?" She sat down on my lap.

"I think so. I mean, you're on my mind all day and night. I'm always happy that you're here when I wake up, even if you're not here when I go to bed. You and my son get along so well, and butterflies form in my stomach whenever you're around. I love everything about you, Jerome Block Winston. From your rude and ignorant comments, to the way you make me scream your name." River and I started kissing and it was like our first time.

"You think, Ryan heard us?" I asked, patting her leg so I could get up.

"Unless he can hear from blocks away, I doubt it. The neighbors may have though." She shrugged making me follow her to the bathroom.

"When did he leave?"

"I told Ryan, I wanted to make love to my man when you went to the store. He packed Jasir up and took him to his house. Ms. Rogers wanted him to stay a few nights anyway." She shut the shower on.

"I didn't know."

"No you didn't because I sucked your dick at the door. That alone should've told you no one was here."

"I thought you were being smart."

"No need to. Ryan respects me and you. Now step in so I can wash all my juices off." Following her directions, I did what she asked.

"Don't hurt me, Block." Her voice was so sincere.

"I won't purposely, but I'll probably mess up and not by having sex with someone. It could be something stupid but I promise not to intentionally hurt you." We kissed again but this time she washed both of us up. Once we dried off, we got in bed naked and passed out.

CHAPTER 5

Chana

"Are you sure about this?" Ryan asked, pulling me close to him. We were at my house because his son was at his place.

I met Ryan a year ago, when me and my father moved to town. We were from this area but due to some family issues, we were separated at one point. I'm still unsure of what took place in my father's life because he didn't want to speak on it, but once we returned he would say a little here and there. He was embarrassed, ashamed and most of all sickened by the events. I would be too if my sister made me do things like that growing up.

Anyway, Ryan was sick and brought himself to the emergency room. I was the nurse on duty that night. He was diagnosed with the flu and told to stay home for a few days like all patients. Days later when he was feeling better, we ran into one another at a park. He had his son there and I was running my laps like usual.

He stopped me while his son played with the other kids but made sure his eyes were on him at all times. I understood because people were snatching kids left and right from their parents. Long story short, we exchanged phone numbers, went out on a few dates and maybe six months later, he allowed me to meet Jasir. He was the sweetest kid ever and he loved his mom and dad.

Ryan never spoke on why he had Jasir a lot. I figured his mom must work so they take turns keeping him. Their co-parenting skills were remarkable if you ask me. Neither of them invaded the others space, they had a great friend relationship and lastly, she didn't want him and vice versa. That's unusual knowing women and men stake claim on one another even after they break up.

The day Jasir was shot, we were at the park discussing if we wanted to move in with one another. Both of us stayed with our parents and since we confessed our love to each other, why not. Ryan was the man of my dreams and he felt the same about me.

Sadly, some idiot came flying down the street out of nowhere and started shooting. You could tell he aimed at the house before the park but because he kept shooting, three kids were hit; including Jasir. Ryan tried his hardest to make it to him but it was too late.

Kids were screaming, and some of the parents out there were running to their cars to leave. Others stayed to help and called for paramedics. My nurse instinct kicked in immediately.

Pushing Ryan off Jasir, I saw the bullet in his leg and had him take his belt off to make a tourniquet. I quickly removed the shoestrings out of Jasir shoes to do the same for his arm.

Once I saw the bleeding stop, I ran over to check the other kids. One was hit on the side and another was hit in his shoulder and it appeared it grazed his face. Blood was everywhere and the screams could probably be heard miles away. Who in their right mind would shoot at a park or around one? Thank goodness, all three kids survived.

When River arrived, something about her was so familiar. She was hysterical and the guy she walked in with had a concerned look on his face. You could tell he either had strong feelings for her or was in love with her. He tried to keep her calm and managed to do it, which would've been impossible for anyone who heard their child was hurt.

I wasn't feeling the way he spoke to my father, yet understood. I'm not sure how long him and River knew one another but I'm positive she mentioned not having a father around, and I blame Louise and Charlene for that. Hearing some man say he was going to visit his girlfriend, regardless aggravated the guy.

When he punched my father, I wanted to say something but it was too many of them there. Ain't no way, they wouldn't have beat my ass. I'm trained in Karate, Jujitsu and I box on occasion at the gym. However, I'm not tryna go to jail and who knew what type of shit they were on.

"I'm ok. Are you ok?" I questioned him. Ever since we found out River was my sister, things became uncomfortable. The man I'm in love with had a child with my biological sister, which made his son my nephew. It was very weird for both of us.

"Yea." He kissed my cheek. That was another thing, it felt forced to even do that much.

"Ok. Let's get this over with." I blew my breath, grabbed my things, and went downstairs to get in my car. He drove his own because he was making a stop at home to check on Jasir. He called wanting to see him.

"Hey, daddy. You there yet?" I asked if he got to the address we were given. I had Ryan speak to River's man and see if he could get us to have a conversation with her. It took two weeks because they were still dealing with Jasir being shot and her health as well.

"I'm here. This house is humongous and it's a bunch of niggas outside smoking." I started laughing. It's probably his family and they're going to try and keep him calm.

"Ok. I'll be there shortly. I'm in the car." We hung up. I took a deep breath because this had been the moment we needed in order to move forward.

"You're River's sister? Damn, good looks just run in y'all family. Wait! Are you as blind as her because she looks crazy with those bifocals on?" A young kid asked when we walked in the house. He didn't appear to be any older than seventeen.

"I am and my eyes are perfectly fine." This young kid had the nerve to lick his lips.

"Boy, get yo ass outta here. You wouldn't know what to do with someone like that." An older gentleman clowned him.

"Pops, don't hate the player. Hate the game." I couldn't help but laugh.

"Don't mind him. He just turned sixteen and I paid this bitch to show him how to fuck. You can't tell him shit now." My mouth fell open. I couldn't believe he just said that.

"I'm Montell." He extended his hand to shake. They were very soft and he was handsome too. Had I not been in love with Ryan, I may have flirted. As long as a man was over the age of twenty one there was no discrimination here.

"Montell don't get this bitch fucked up fantasizing about you." Some woman walked in with an attitude. The entire family must be rude. He pulled her into his body and just like that, she melted.

"Ain't nobody getting this dick but you." Those two started kissing.

"You can come in here." A younger woman spoke. She was gorgeous and you could tell she was pregnant due to her belly poking out.

"Hi, I'm Arabia. That is my mother, Janetta."

"Ugh, why you tell them my name? What if they the OPPs. I may have warrants out there." My dad shook his head.

"There is my father, my other brother Onyx, my cousin, Mariah and you know, Block and River." He stood in front of River so I wasn't able to see her yet. I did at the hospital but with so much chaos going on, I never got a good look. As she went on with the introductions, it felt like all eyes were on us.

"Remind me again why we agreed to meet here?" My father tried to whisper.

"You're here because River don't know either of you, and since y'all family fucked up, we had to make sure wasn't no funny shit going down." The woman who was introduced as Mariah blurted out. I understood exactly what she meant. I'm glad they were here for her because Louise wasn't no role model.

"Block, move out her way. Damn, y'all been hugged up since you got here." Arabia spoke with aggravation in her voice.

"That's because she done strung that nigga out. He ain't been like that since his crackhead ex was having orgys and giving out HIV." I was flabbergasted at his mother's outburst. Then again, it's obvious this family says anything.

"Whatever." Block turned around and I saw exactly how handsome he was. Dressed in a green Nike sweatsuit with Jordans to match let me know he could most likely dress. The Diamond necklace he wore shined brightly, as well as the Diamond studs in his ear that were huge too.

"Hi. I'm River." She made her way around Block and to us. My father immediately teared up.

"I'm Chana and he is our father." She shook our hands. I told my dad not to expect a kumbaya moment because she doesn't know us.

"Are you thirsty?" River offered us a drink.

"Block, tell Velma not to offer hospitality to people we don't know and she didn't pay for no drinks over here." River rolled her eyes at his mother.

"Velma?" Me and my dad were both confused.

"Don't mind his mom. She gets like that when the crabs make her itch."

"Oh, you little heffa. Now I done told you about telling my business. And for the record, you sat on the toilet after me so guess who had them now." Right then I knew they were joking. Everyone shook their heads at the two of them.

"Can we talk in private?" My dad asked.

"This nigga." Block made sure to let us hear him.

"It's ok, Babe. You can stay if you want but Janetta can't." His father escorted her out and everyone followed, except Block, Onyx and his mother. I'm not sure why they stayed but since my father didn't oppose, I'm not either.

"Is your son here?" My dad glanced around.

"You lucky you here. Now get to asking questions or telling her what's going on so you can bounce." Block had no filter and he definitely didn't hide his disdain for us being here.

"Excuse us for a minute." River grabbed Block's hand and stepped out the room. I felt my phone vibrate and looked to see it was Ryan saying he would be here soon. I sure hope so because this family was off the hook.

"Ok. We're back." Whatever she said to him, obviously calmed him down. He sat her on his lap and wrapped his arms around her waist.

"Let me start from the beginning." My father said making himself comfortable on the couch. I hope that he would reveal everything because I'm still unsure of a lotta things myself.

!!!!!! Trigger Warning !!!!!!

Please be advised that the content in the following chapter may be disturbing due to a sensitive subject regarding incest, abuse, rape & sodomy. It will contain traumatic scenarios and sexual experiences that some may not want to read.

If you do decide to skip this chapter, it won't take away from the book.

The story will continue with no lapse in it.

Thanks!!

CHAPTER 6

River

"**B**abe, please relax. I need to know whatever it is he wanted to tell me." I pulled Block out the room because he was about to go off.

He explained how he punched this man that claimed to be my father in the face at the hospital. However, if he was who he saying he was, then I had questions and he was the only one with the answers.

"I'll only calm down if you do those tricks on my dick later." I started laughing.

"Fine but that's only because you promised to go half on the seats in my van." We kissed and went to join them in the living room.

"I'm Ernie and this is your fraternal twin, Chana." Block and Onyx sat up quick.

"Excuse me." Me and Chana spoke at the same time. The

woman didn't look anything like me. I guess that's why he said fraternal.

"I know. It's hard to understand so I'm going to walk you through it." Noticing Arabia and Mariah at the door leading into the kitchen, I told them to come in.

My life was an open book so nothing he was about to tell me would be a secret; especially with Janetta sitting on a bar stool chair from the mini bar behind me. That woman was a piece of work but she was growing on me.

"Charlene Buggs is my older sister by five years." He confessed.

"Hold up. That means you and River are cousins." Mariah said what I was thinking.

"Yes they are." Onyx mother sat there quietly. From what Block told me, she had no idea Ernie even existed.

"All our life, Charlene was a bully to me and Louise. We had to do whatever she said or she would beat us whenever our parents left the house, and I'm not talking with her hands. She'd find sticks from outside, thick belts from my father's room and one time she used a bat on my legs."

"What?" Chana yelled.

"At the age of ten, she broke my leg with it because I refused to get her snacks out the kitchen. When my mother asked what happened, I lied and said I fell down the steps." I'm not acquainted with Charlene and to be honest, I'm happy about it.

"Anyway, when my sister, Louise was twelve and I was four-teen, she decided we needed to do something for her. As she says, *"It was a fetish she saw online and wanted us to act it out."* Onyx mother gasped and he turned his face up. Did they already know?

"This is hard to speak on." Ernie stiffened up and started rocking back and forth. He stared at the ceiling for a few minutes.

"What's wrong with him?" I asked Chana who appeared to be just as lost.

"I'm not sure. Dad are you ok?" She rubbed his back and he stopped. The doorbell rang and once Ryan stepped in, I knew she called him to be here for her. Block nodded as if he expected his appearance. Ernie got himself together and continued with the story.

"My father enjoyed hunting and often took, Charlene with him. Louise was terrified of guns and I was into sports. I was always at practice or at a friend's house in order to stay away because my sister was hell on wheels. I blamed my father because he had a severe hand problem and Charlene witnessed a lot." I rested my body on Block. It felt like what he was about to say would be too much to handle.

"You ok?" He whispered.

"Yes, for now." He wrapped his arms around me.

"One afternoon, my mom had to be taken to the hospital due to my father almost killing her. He went along to make sure she didn't blame him and say it was a robbery. I still remember my mother on the ground screaming for help. I tried to get to her but he choked me until I passed out." Damn, my alleged grandfather was a piece of shit.

"When I woke up, Charlene had one of my father's hunting guns on Louise. She was in the corner with her knees to her chest crying and shaking her head no." Not knowing what was going on, I got up slowly and crawled to Louise.

We were very close and even went to our guidance counselor months before requesting to be removed from the home. Unfortunately, when the workers came for a house visit there were no sign of abuse so they left us there. My father beat me real bad for that." He shook his head.

"Charlene told Louise if she didn't agree, she would kill our mother. Still unsure of what was going on, I tried to get the gun out of my sister's hand but being weak from my father choking me, it didn't work."

"I don't want to hear anymore." We all looked at Onyx's mother.

"Shit, I do. Julio, take your wife outta here. This is getting good." Janetta was a mess. Once Ms. Buggs was out the room he continued.

"She forced me and Louise to drink some of my father's liquor. I think it was Whiskey and I can't even name the other one." Ryan was rubbing Chana's shoulders.

"Long story short, Charlene had me and Louise do things to one another that only lovers do." I immediately started vomiting.

"Oh, hell no. That shit better not be stuck in my rug." Janetta yelled. Block helped me in the bathroom and stayed until I calmed down. I rinsed my mouth out with mouthwash and cleaned my face. When we came out, Ernie continued speaking.

"We didn't really know at first because we were so drunk, we passed out. This happened a few times and each time we would be intoxicated, and couldn't remember anything. I think she was putting stuff in the drinks beforehand." I didn't want to hear anymore but I didn't want to leave.

"The one time I did remember, was because the liquor hadn't taken affect yet. I was still groggy and thought I was seeing things."

"What do you mean seeing things?" Chana questioned.

"Charlene was using her hands to get me aroused, and I saw her lifting Louise on top of me. Before you ask, Louise was a small and petite woman like, River and Chana, and as you see, Charlene was a thick woman and she was big back then as well." I was so disgusting listening to this but it gave me insight on why my mother was the way she was.

"Unfortunately, Charlene hit me over the head with something and I passed out." My so called aunt was really crazy.

"One day Louise was sick as hell. Vomiting everywhere, and she couldn't keep anything down. When my mother was well enough, she took her to the doctor. He told Louise she was pregnant and my sister cried because she had never had sex. I'm not thinking about what I saw Charlene do because before she knocked me out, I pushed Louise off me."

"Nooooo." Chana dragged the word out.

"Louise was so distraught because she had no idea who she was pregnant by. That was until Charlene showed videos of us doing things we shouldn't have been. One would assume being that drunk we wouldn't be able get it on, but that wasn't the truth. Charlene made it happen by may means necessary. Shit, she was the one who told us the baby was mine." The story was getting crazier by the minute.

"Like I said, we were passed out so she orchestrated everything, even breaking my sisters virginity with a sex toy. The way she laughed seeing my sister bleed was wicked."

"She wasn't hurting the next day?" I asked because after me and Ryan had sex the first time, it took me some time to do it again, That pain was bad.

"Louise told my mother about the pain but she brushed it aside and told her it could be cramps. Louise tried to explain the feeling but like I said, my mother wasn't listening." He explained.

"That's fucking disgusting." Mariah responded to what he said.

"I refuse to go into detail on how she did other things but just know Charlene was the devil."

"Damn!" Arabia whispered as she listened. Block was holding me up because I started dry heaving.

"It took years of therapy to finally admit that I had kids that were also my nieces." He let the tears fall.

"Child services removed us from the home for the time being after finding out what really took place. Unfortunately, they put us back because Charlene moved out so the threat was gone." He sounded devastated telling the story.

"Seeing Louise pregnant with my kids took a toll on me and I ran away. I started stealing from stores just to be arrested so I'd have somewhere to stay. Thankfully, after a few more times, I went to a group home." You could hear the hurt in his voice.

"My counselor told me, Louise had twins and one stayed in the hospital due to having RSV." He pointed to Chana.

"She tried to leave, River but my mother wouldn't allow it. She never blamed Louise after learning the truth, and she didn't want her grandkids in foster care regardless of how they were conceived."

"That's why she always called me an abomination and tried to kill my son. We reminded her of what, Charlene made her do." I told him what Louise had always said to me.

"Why didn't she get an abortion?" Arabia asked.

"My mother didn't believe in those and because we were kids, we had no authority to go alone."

"Damn. That's wild." Ryan now spoke up.

"The only reason why the two of them were split up was because my grandmother moved them away soon as my sister came home from the hospital. When they tried to reach out for her to get, Chana, they were gone. The cops went to the house and saw it was still in a livable condition but they were nowhere to be found."

"Which was how we ended up here." Chana chimed in.

"Wait! I thought y'all were from this area." Ryan said to Chana.

"We were from here as kids but when she left with Louise, we never heard from her. I guess after my mother died when we were eighteen, Louise decided to come back." Everyone was quiet and in their own heads.

"How did you find me and how did you find Chana?" He held her hand.

"The group home asked me if I wanted my sister's daughter because she ran off. At first, I said no but after learning Chana could be lost in the system forever and I may never find her, I kept her. How could I let my daughter slash niece go in foster care?" He smiled at her.

"The group home placed me with a family who took in young fathers. They were really nice and helped me a lot." He explained how they taught him how to care for a young child alone.

"At eighteen, I was informed of my mother's death. Unfortunately, my father had beat her to death and killed himself right after."

"Damn, y'all family had a lot going on." Mariah spoke out loud.

"The system actually worked for me and Chana by giving me housing, childcare and food stamps. I thought I'd be ashamed as a man with stamps but I wasn't."

"I wouldn't have been able to do it." Onyx said, shaking his head.

"Trust me it was the hardest decision of my life but she made me a better person. Chana was the reason I continued therapy, got a degree in psychology, and learned how to love a woman." He explained how he was married with three sons but didn't want to introduce them until he knew for sure I'd be ok with it.

"When your son was shot, Ryan called you on the phone.

Chana heard him say your name and how ironic was it for someone to have that exact name. I rushed to get there in hopes that it was you and I'm glad I did." Not knowing what to say, I remained quiet.

"Wait a minute!" Onyx spoke.

"At the hospital you acted as if you didn't know, Charlene had kids. How was that possible when she was only thirteen?"

"I see my sister left a lot out." He retorted.

"We didn't know Charlene was pregnant, not even my parents. When she turned six months my father figured it out and sent her to live with our grandmother. She returned a few months later with no baby. My father told us she had a stillborn child and not to ever bring it up again. Since my sister didn't talk about it when she returned, we assumed it was true."

"Wow!" I was at a loss for words.

"You have to remember, at the time she was thirteen, I was eight and Louise was six. We didn't ask questions at that age." Everyone nodded.

"I'm sorry you had to find out but I'm happy to have found you." I wanted to hug him but my body was stuck under Block. I didn't want to move nor did I want anyone to speak to me.

"Now what?" Onyx asked no one in particular.

"Welp, you found out you're related to, River and Chana. And you learned the truth about your grandmother." He didn't say anything. Mariah reached her hands out for him to stand with her. They ended up leaving.

"I guess that's our cue to leave as well." Chana stood and helped Ernie.

"Go ahead, I'll be right out." Ryan yelled as they left.

"River, I didn't know she was your sister. I wouldn't do that to you." Block squeezed my leg to let me know he was about to say something. It's what I asked him to do earlier if something bothered him.

"Ryan, if you're in love with her, I'm ok with that. Like you said, neither of you knew and we were only friends."

"Yea but—"

"Nigga, she don't care and neither do I. As long as you not tryna fuck, River, we good." Block butted in.

"What? Hell no. I consider River more of my sister than anything." Did he just say that?

"Excuse me." I couldn't believe Ryan.

"River don't get fucked up."

"Anyway, Ryan. I could tell she loves you. Treat her right and make sure she treats, Jasir right because if she doesn't, he will tell." He laughed. I gave him a hug and Block was about to lose it. I walked Ryan to the door and waved goodbye to Ernie and Chana who were still outside.

"Trust me, Block. He doesn't want me." I sat on his lap facing forward with my knees on the couch. Everyone gave us privacy.

"I only want you so remember that when you see me speaking to any guy."

"Whatever." The two of us started kissing.

"Little girl, I know your knees not in my couch and you not tryna fuck my son." I rolled my eyes at Janetta and got up.

"Been there, done that and besides, the shit we do behind

closed doors would make you think we're porn stars." Block laughed.

"Ok, Miss Flowers in the Attic." What the hell did that mean?

"Flowers in the Attic?" I was confused.

"You don't know the movie where the brother and sister had sex because the grandmother kept them locked away in the attic so her daughter could be a ho." She mentioned some movie.

"What?"

"Yup, they had three kids too. The only difference was your aunt made them do it. Do you think she locked them in a room when their parents was gone?"

"Bye."

"Wait! Do you think she had flowers in the room when they did it?" Janetta was getting on my nerves now.

"A'ight, Ma. That's enough." Block moved her away from me.

"River." I stopped at the door.

"I'm sorry that your family fucked up like that and your dad is your uncle." I swung the door open. She did try and be sentimental but sarcasm always came behind it.

"But if you ever need a mother figure in your life, my door will not be open. I don't like your ass." I looked at Block and busted out laughing. Even though she pissed me off, I appreciated her trying to make me laugh. Walking over to Janetta, I hugged her tight. Shockingly, she held onto me.

"Don't let what, Charlene did keep you from getting to

know your father. He made the first move so make sure you at least try." She kissed my forehead and pushed me hard as hell into Block.

"Now get out! I don't even hug my own kids." Block lifted me up and carried me to the truck.

"You ok?"

"I think I am. Knowing the truth put a lot of things in perspective for me." He kissed me before putting me down.

"I'm here for whatever you need." The two of us got in and drove to see Jasir. Ms. Rogers welcomed Block with open arms and we stayed over for a couple of hours. Jasir wasn't ready to come home. I did bathe and get him ready for bed before we left. I'm glad this day was over.

CHAPTER 7
Mariah

The day we left my aunt's house after hearing what Charlene did, all we did was go home. Onyx didn't want to speak with anyone or eat anything. He showered and waited for me to lie next to him before dosing off. I'm surprised he was able to rest because my ass was up all night going over the things his alleged uncle stated.

To my knowledge, Chana sent River a message that night asking if they were able to go to Lab Corp for them all to do a DNA test. No one assumed they were lying but it would put all of them at ease to know the truth.

At first, Ms. Buggs refused and I think it's because she didn't want to know the truth. Whatever happened in the past she wanted to keep it there. Even I know until you deal with something head on there won't be any closure. I learned that from my mother and now with my husband. Holding things in can cause problems and I've witnessed it firsthand dealing with some of the issues regarding Onyx and the other women.

I knew about the chicks he crept off with when we got into arguments. I'm aware of the two chicks whose bills he paid as well as the back and forth with Salina. The pregnancy scares were fake, as well as some of the women saying he was with them, yet he was lying next to me. Women go through a lot of unnecessary drama to keep a man in their life and I'm not afraid to admit that was me.

Onyx Buggs was the man of my dreams and he wasn't going anywhere. If that meant dealing with other women, then it was what it was. Some may consider it being a weak woman but not me. See, men take forever to grow up and don't know how to deal with one woman at a time. You have to show them that you can do everything they can. Onyx may not be aware of me stepping out but you can believe I had my share of being with another man when we broke up.

Sean was a guy from the gym who worked as a trainer. He had the body most men stayed in the gym to get and his dick did some good things for me. He knew how to make me cum hard and his pussy eating was amazing. After having sex with him, my appetite for that hood loving only came from Onyx.

I anticipated going to the gym and once my session was over, we'd creep off. We'd meet up at a hotel, do our thing and go on with our life until the next time. Onyx had no clue because not only was he working, he was too busy tryna keep his ho's in line. To this day, that was the only secret I held from him. Sean and I continued for a couple of months. We only stopped because we both had someone and feelings were starting to surface.

We as women don't always have to share what we've done. Just knowing we had that spade to play at any time was enough for us to deal with the bullshit. A nigga will always lose his mind when he finds out a woman did what he did, and that's the best part.

"Let me talk to you." Onyx pulled me out the kitchen. River and Block were sitting on the couch talking. *When did they even get here?*

"Hey." I spoke. Block walked over to hug me while River kept her head in the phone. We were cordial with one another but that was as far as it went.

"What you doing here?"

"It's been brought to our attention that you two don't fuck with each other." River lifted her head. She was as confused as me.

"I have no idea what you're talking about." Did she mention how we didn't speak?

"Look, I don't give a fuck what happened at the salon. She is my cousin and—"

"Alleged." I corrected him. Onyx chuckled. Block was shaking his head and River sat there being a mute.

"You think that nigga stopped by to make up a lie about him being my uncle or that he told a story about incest just because. What would he gain from that? Do you have any idea how hard that was for him to admit to that, and for us to hear?"

He shut me right up.

"Like I said, she is my cousin, and you're my wife. Y'all damn sure don't have to ever fuck with one another. However, ain't gonna be no rolling eyes at each other, or talking shit about the other." He spoke sternly about the situation.

"You don't even know her; none of y'all do and all of a sudden I'm supposed to bite my tongue around her."

"This the shit I be talking about, Mariah." I felt myself becoming angry.

"No one said you had to fuck with her at all and vice versa. You hear what you wanna hear." He started to get aggravated.

"Mariah, come outside real quick." Block grabbed my hand and led me to the back. He closed the door.

"We know what happened at the salon between you two." He leaned on the outside wall.

"Oh yea! What did she say?"

"Honestly, she wasn't the one who brought it up. When I asked her about it, she said it was over and done with. You had a bad day and she moved on from it." He put his hands on top of my shoulders.

"You're not the first person who gave her shit at the salon and won't be the last." People do treat others how they want.

"Then why is he bringing it up." My eyes began to water.

"Mariah, all of their worlds have just been turned upside down. The shit they've been told was like a Lifetime movie. They have new family members now and all Onyx wanted was his wife to be stress free."

"But—"

"But you're giving him a hard time for nothing. And before you ask, no River had no idea this was why we came either. I told her we stopped by for me to talk to him." I wiped my eyes. He hugged me.

"He didn't want to have new family members around unless his wife was comfortable." He pulled away to look at me.

"We just don't want no friction between you two. Well, you anyway because she barely speaks."

"I can't tell." He laughed.

"She speaks with the people she's comfortable with. Remember at the diner, she started opening up to the family but then we got the phone call about her son." I do recall having general conversation with her but that's because everyone chimed in on whatever we spoke about.

"Mariah, her son was shot and she just found out she's a product of incest." I turned my nose up.

"Shit, I'm still dealing with hearing that too. What if we ever have kids; will the kid be deformed? Then again, Jasir good." We took a seat in one of the chairs.

"Mariah stop fighting Onyx on everything. That man is in love with you and would lay his life on the line for you, we all know that."

"I know." I laid my head against the chair and closed my eyes.

"I'm not sure how long, River will be in my life but as of right now, she not going nowhere." I opened my eyes quickly.

"You love her." He shrugged.

"She's in love with me and I'm not tryna fuck up in case what I'm feeling is love and not lust. Shit it's been almost a year since, Leslie." He was in love with her and took it hard when she left him over the mess with Avery. They always say men are no good but we all know *Every Block Boy Needs A Little Love* too.

"If you wanna be mad at someone, be mad at Arabia because she brought it up." I sucked my teeth.

"Arabia wants all of us to get along and you already know with Deray being alive, she needs you around for support."

"Why don't she ask her new bestie, River to support her?" He busted out laughing.

"Is that jealousy seeping out?" He joked.

"River and Arabia have become close, yes but she'll never be as close as you and Arabia so stop it." He helped me out the chair.

"Again, no one was trying to force you to friends. We just don't want you beefing with her." I agreed to remain cordial. We walked back in the house and heard laughing. Onyx and River were on the couch together. If they weren't related, I'd have a major problem with them being that close.

"Babe, Onyx said you're scared of spiders. He showed me this video of you two at work where you were running from one." River stood to show him the phone.

"Bro, you play too damn much. I told you to erase that." Onyx shrugged.

"It's ok. I'm not afraid of spiders. I'll save you if we see one." River made a joke.

"She can't come around you no more." Block snapped making me laugh.

"You ready." River grabbed her things and stopped next to me.

"We don't ever have to be friends, Mariah. As long as you respect me, I will do the same." She peeked around to speak with Onyx.

"I want to see more videos or hear more stories about my new, Bae one day."

"I got you." Onyx answered as the two of them walked toward the door. When it closed, he patted the top of his lap for me to sit.

"You're so fucking spoiled it's ridiculous." I rolled my eyes as he made me face him. My stomach was really out there but he always made it work when he wanted me close.

"My husband made me this way." He moved the hair out my face.

"Nah, you been like that but I take responsibility for making it worse." He ripped my shirt open, unsnapped my bra and sucked on my tender breasts.

"Take those sweats off." I stood to do what he said. When he licked his lips, I knew he was about to take what he wanted.

"Lift your leg up here." He kissed up my thigh, then had me sit on his erect dick that he pulled out his sweats.

"My wife has the best pussy in the world. Fuck!" He moaned and leaned back to watch me go up and down.

"If you ever fuck another nigga, I'm gonna kill you this time." I froze. Did he know? Why did he say that?

"Damn, she wet as fuck." Trying not to let what he said bother me, I pushed it out my head because he was doing amazing things to my body.

After we finished, he led me upstairs to shower. I wanted to address his comment so bad but decided against it. We just had a great sex session, why sour the mood with something he said in the heat of the moment. Now that I think about it, he didn't know. If he did, he would've called me out on it, or left me.

I laid in the bed next to him telling myself I'm taking that shit to the grave. It may be a spade for me to use but my life depended on it too. With my daughter on the way, it wasn't worth hurting him that bad.

"Why don't you listen when I talk to you?" My mother chastised me as we sat in her living room. I had a doctor's appointment today and afterwards, I had Onyx bring me here to get advice.

"Ma, he didn't say he knew." I explained what Onyx said yesterday. Of course I'll never tell her it was during sex.

"Mariah, what is wrong with you? You can't read between the lines."

"Ugh, no." I had my feet propped up on the couch.

"He said and I'm quoting what you said, *If you do it again,*

I'll kill you this time." The way she replayed it did imply that he knew.

"It sounds clear as day to me." My mother fussed going in the kitchen.

"Why didn't he just say it then?" I wasn't backing down from my feelings. If he knew, then why wasn't he telling me.

"Did it ever occur to you that he wanted to hear you say it? Maybe he wanted to apologize for the hurt he caused you and would understand why you did it." What she said made sense but again, Onyx wasn't the type of man to be ok with a woman stepping out on him; especially me.

"He already apologized a million times."

"Mariah, I don't see this going well." She held my hand in hers after taking a seat next to me.

"You hated when he had secrets but you're holding in one of your own." She's right but

his secrets nearly destroyed us.

"I'm not telling him." She snatched her hand away.

"Ok. Do not and I repeat, do not bring your ass over here crying when he finds out. I don't wanna hear it. I washed my hands." She swiped her hands up and down as if she were doing it.

"Not doing what?" My father stepped in the room.

"Tell him, Mariah." My dad stood there waiting for me to answer. I hated that his stare could force me to speak. My mother was tapping her feet against the marble floor irritating the hell out of me.

"I slept with someone else and never told, Onyx. It was only with one person and—" I blurted out.

"How many times?" He cut me off.

"It was with the same guy."

"How many times?" He repeated the question.

"A lot." He swiped his hand down his face.

"That nigga gonna kill you, then I gotta deal with Block and Montell for killing him." He didn't yell or shout. Block loved Onyx like his brother and Montell considered him, his nephew.

"Daddy, it happened when he cheated on me." He sat across from me folding his hands.

"As shallow as it may sound, it's different when a woman stepped out." I tried to tell him again it was on a break but he cut me off.

"You stuck by him each time he cheated, which I thought was dumb but hey, that was your relationship." I nodded.

"However, if you felt the need for revenge, and that's what it was no matter how you try and sugar coat it, you should've left him alone."

"I couldn't."

"You caught feelings for that other man, didn't you?" My head went down in shame.

"Risking another man's life for revenge was low, Mariah, even for you." He wasn't happy.

"Daddy."

"If he wasn't already killed, he will be." My dad stood up with frustration on his face.

"No. I was extra careful with him." Why did they both laugh?

"You weren't ready for marriage." He walked away disappointed. My mother was just as disgusted with me. The only thing left for me to do was leave. Instead of calling Onyx, I asked Arabia to get me. I'll go home later.

CHAPTER 8

Arabia

"He's getting big, Arabia." The doctor said, showing me, DJ on the screen. It took everything in me to keep him as a Junior after finding out Deray faked his death.

"Thanks. I've been eating a lot better."

"I see. Your weight has increased as well. What changed?" She removed the device off my stomach and printed me a sonogram photo.

I was very open with my doctor and she knew I wasn't taking care of myself once Deray died. Hunger pains barely came to me and dehydration set in a few times. At the time, all I wanted to do was be with Deray again. Now that he was back, I wanted nothing to do with him.

He called nonstop, sent text messages, showed up at the house too many times to count, and even sent some of the videos we took. Flowers, cards and candy would arrive every

Saturday and Sunday with cards that read, *"I'm sorry."* But was he? How could he be when everyone besides me knew he was alive? I hated that he did this to us.

"It could be the fact that my son's father was alive after all." I continued putting my clothes on.

"Really?" She was surprised. I sat on the table and explained what took place, minus the fact Deray was out to get Huff. She didn't need to know the ins and outs of the shooting nor was it my place to tell her. All she knew was my man got shot, he died and came back to life; the end.

"Wow. At least he'll be around for the delivery." I laughed at her comment.

"Honestly, he can stay dead." I shrugged, gathering my things up to leave. We said our goodbyes and she went to her office, while I went to my car. I took a photo of the sonogram picture and sent it to Deray. It's the least I could do since he threatened to kill me if I kept him away.

Deray: *What the fuck, Arabia*

Me: *I'm not sure I know what you mean*

Deray: *Why didn't you tell me about the doctor's appointment? I told you I wanted to be*

there.

Me: *Oh, you were there spiritually, just not physically. Remember you're always with me. That's what your mother said.* I could see the bubbles pop up like he was responding. I quickly went to his name, clicked edit and hit block. He needs to know how it felt to not know what was going on.

* * *

"Hey, how you feeling?" River asked, coming in my mother's house. Block brought her by to do my hair. Deray was calling me from unknown numbers threatening to kill me if I didn't answer him, and since I'm not trying to die right now, I'm just going to stay here until my delivery.

"I'm ok. How are you? How's Jasir?" She followed me in the downstairs bedroom where she did my hair the first time.

"He's getting better. The doctor removed the cast off his arm but the one on his leg will remain. It's taking a lot longer to heal." I couldn't imagine what she was going through as a parent and didn't want to. One thing I can say was River is a strong woman.

In my opinion it's the exact reason Block was falling for her. She didn't expect anyone to give her anything and before the housing came through, she made things work for her and her son. Block always admired women who went and got things on their own without looking for handouts or giving excuses.

"I heard my mom gave you a hug."

"You're not upset are you? Block told me she didn't do that a lot with you two." River wrapped the cape around my neck to wash my hair. It was a regular bathroom sink and the cape was from the beauty supply store. If I couldn't get to the shop, why not bring the supplies here.

"What? No. My mother is emotional and whether she said it or not, she really felt bad about your family's situation." She spoke to me about it in private and said she would've killed Charlene on the spot if it were one of us. Just don't expect another one unless something bad happens." I joked.

River decided to stay even longer after doing my hair. Her and my mother went back and forth as usual. Once she left, I did go to McDonald's because I wanted a milkshake. Slowly getting out my car, this nigga was standing right there.

"When the fuck did you get pregnant?" Hearing his voice made me turn around and get right back in. Thankfully, I hadn't walked inside the place. Knowing Huff, he would've blocked me in.

"How many months are you?" He wouldn't allow me to close the door.

"Why? It's not your baby." A smile appeared on his face.

"It could be mine now since that nigga dead." He folded his arms and stood in a spot that still wouldn't allow me to close the door.

"You killed him?" I pretended not to know the truth.

"Hell yea. My bitch was sneaking off every night to fuck. Why wouldn't I?"

"Huff, we weren't even a couple. You were sleeping with different women."

"I don't care! You were my woman; that's supposed to be my kid in your stomach." It was time for me to deescalate the situation. Huff had a way of as he says, blacking out and I don't have the strength or energy to fight back.

"Huff don't do this." I tried to close the door.

"Do what? Huh? I should beat your ass." And just like that,

his handed connected with my face. Blood seeped out my mouth as another fist caught me in the eye.

"You're not having this baby." I saw him lift his foot and prepared myself for the inevitable. I couldn't close the door and he was too strong for me to push him away.

"Aye, yo. What you doing?" I heard a voice but didn't know who it was.

"Help me!" I screamed.

"I'm gonna kill you, bitch." Huff ran off and the guy came to my aide.

"Got dammit. That nigga gonna lose it." He ran around the car and grabbed some napkins out the glove compartment.

"Yo, call 911." He told a woman coming out.

"I'm fine."

"Sis, you are not fine. Your eye is almost closed and blood is pouring out your mouth. I would say he broke your jaw but he couldn't have if you're talking." The woman stood outside the car describing my injuries to the 911 people.

"I just want to go home." He refused to let me leave. Once the EMT's came, I was taken to the hospital again. This time it was closer to home however, I wasn't expecting my entire family to show up. Block and Onyx was so mad, my father had to escort them out to calm down.

"I know he's been around the family for years but he gotta go." My Uncle Montell said rubbing the side of my face. As we sat there talking, I smelled him come in. That cologne of his was so distinct, I always knew when he was around.

"Can I talk to her alone?" How did he know where I was?

"You look good for a dead nigga." My mother said, giving him the death stare.

"My apologies for making her hurt."

"Yea, yea. Next time you play dead, tell your shady ass family to stay away too. We don't play that phony shit." Deray shook his head and pulled a chair up next to me.

"How you feeling?" I turned over.

"Arabia, I don't care how long you stay mad at me. Just tell me you and my son are ok." Why was he asking and he could see with his own eyes that we were.

"How did you know where I was?" He chuckled.

"After you played me out the other day with the doctor's appointment. I put someone on you." I turned back over.

"He thought you were talking to the guy. As you know when he made it to you, the guy ran off." He wiped the tears coming down. I loved this man with all my heart and he hurt me.

"I have an idea who it was but I need you to verify it." All I did was nod my head yes. He lifted the phone from his pocket and made a call.

"It's a go." He disconnected the call and focused back on me.

"I know you're gonna make me suffer and I'm cool with that. Just promise you won't make me miss another appointment."

"How can I when I'm being watched?"

"Touché. Oh, the locks on your door were changed."

"Why?"

"If I was able to kick it off the hinges then someone else could too." I smiled.

"Ok, Miss Winston." The doctor walked in to tell me if I could leave or not.

"Nah, it's Miss Smith." He corrected the doctor by adding his last name.

"It says—"

"I don't give a fuck what it says. Her name is, Miss Smith." The doctor looked at me. I nodded in order not to cause any friction.

"Well, you lost two teeth on the side which I'm sure you know." Deray started to ball up his fist.

"Your eye will heal on its own and as you can see, the baby is fine. I do recommend bed rest for the remainder of the pregnancy." He said a few more things and walked out. One of the nurses stepped in to unhook the monitors.

"You need help getting dressed?"

"No, she doesn't. I got her." The nurse stepped out quickly, closing the door behind her.

Deray grabbed my clothes and walked over to me. I stood with my back facing him. He removed the gown and placed a kiss on my collarbone, then my neck. My nipples were becoming hard and his touch was gentle, yet soothing.

"When you're ready for me to come home, let me know." He cupped my breast and massaged them tenderly. A soft moan escaped my lips.

"Deray." I managed to get out right before he turned my body around and slid his tongue in my mouth.

"Sit here." He grabbed one of the chairs and placed it in front of the door under the handle.

"What are you doing?" Grabbing the bed remote, he made the bed rise to his waist. He pushed my legs up, pulled down his jeans and boxers and slowly went in.

"I missed you, Arabia."

"Same here." I wrapped my legs around his body and thrusted my pelvis into his. I couldn't believe we were having sex in the hospital room.

"You can't keep making me wait for sex. I'm cumming too fast." His fingers went to circle my clit and a few minutes later we were climaxing together.

"I love you, Deray but I need time." Grabbing some tissues off the tray table they had in here, he wiped himself down, lifted his boxers and jeans.

"I love you too and I know." He helped me in the bathroom to wash up. I made him do the same.

The nurse came ten minutes later with the discharge papers and we were on our way downstairs. Block was waiting for me, smirking at Deray.

"You went all out for my sister." Deray didn't say a word. Block was parked at the exit door waiting for me with the window down.

"Let me know when you at your mom's." We kissed before he went to his car.

"What did he go all out for?" I asked Block when he drove out the parking lot. He started laughing.

"That nigga had someone take out Huff's parents, who

happened to be at the house when they went looking for him. When they finished, the house exploded." I gasped.

"That nigga fucked up bad, Sis but he loves you." He thought it was funny.

"What about, Huff?"

"Don't worry. He won't bother you again."

"Did y'all catch him?"

"Not yet. Huff crazy but he knows there's no coming back from this. He won't return but trust and believe, we will find him." I guess that was some reassurance but what if he did return.

CHAPTER 9

Onyx

"Wow, so y'all are really related." Mariah appeared to be shocked by the lab results that arrived in the mail today.

"What's the problem?"

Ever since my Uncle Ernie showed up on the scene and revealed all that information, it seemed as if Mariah wasn't happy. I'm not sure if it was because she snapped on River at the salon for no reason or that Arabia was spending time with River. Whatever the case it was petty as hell to me.

"Nothing." She placed the paper on the table. As I stared down at her, I could tell something was on her mind. She wasn't being her normal uppity wife that walked around with her head held high. She stayed home a lot now and only came out the room to eat or go to the doctors.

I was thrown off when she asked me to pick her up from Arabia's, especially since I dropped her off at her parents. Whatever was bothering her would come out eventually because she didn't know how to keep anything away from me. No matter how much she tried, I always knew.

"I can't tell. As of lately, you've been snapping at everyone, catching attitudes for minor things and if I'm being completely honest, your sex is mediocre." I shrugged not caring about hurting her feelings.

"Onyx, I'm pregnant."

"Mariah, I appreciate you going out your way during the pregnancy to make sure I'm satisfied. But I'm talking about after the gender reveal. You basically just lay there unless I move your body." I know my wife's stomach was huge now but before that, she started slacking in the bedroom. I'm all for her being tired, restless, and uncomfortable, but to say you want to sleep and still sit up all night watching movies or playing games on her phone, that's where the confusion came in for me.

"I just have things on my mind." I remained quiet to see if she'd speak on it. She hated to sit in silence.

"Onyx, I have to tell you something." There it was, but my phone started to ring just before she finished. It was River and I saw another number pop up too, which meant someone was on three way.

"One sec, Mariah. What's up, River and who on the phone?" I gave her my phone number when she stopped by with Block. In a sense we knew we were related. No one was going to show up describing what they went through to complete strangers. Not only that, Charlene verified who Ernie was at the hospital.

"Heyyyyy, cousin." She sang in the phone.

"Hi, Onyx. It's Chana and we were calling to see if you received the results too." They were very excited.

"I did."

"You think it's too early for a family reunion. I mean, it's obvious we have a big family now." River was excited as she spoke which made me smile.

After hearing the things she went through from Block it's to be expected. Chana didn't have it nowhere near as bad as her sister, shit who would want to.

"So, you're just gonna sit on the phone with that bitch when we were in the middle of a conversation?" I turned to Mariah and she jumped after seeing my face. Why would my wife feel the need to be disrespectful to a woman who had not said one bad thing about her?

"Oh, we're sorry, Onyx. We had no idea you were busy." Chana said. I could tell it was her because her voice was deeper and raspy.

"Onyx, I'm overjoyed that we're related but I'm telling you now, I'm not going to be any more bitches for your wife." River snapped as she should have. Mariah was loud as hell.

"I'm quiet and respectful, but I can tell you, I'm not a soft bitch. If she continues to call me out my name, we will have a problem."

"I respect that. Let me call y'all back." River had every right to feel the way she did. Hopefully it won't ever come down to them throwing hands because that's where it'll become a problem for me.

"Y'all?" Mariah blurted out. I disconnected the call, grabbed my keys, and headed to the door. The amount of anger building up in me was enough to hurt her feelings real bad and possibly leave her.

"So, you're just gonna walk out while we were talking." Ignoring her, I opened the door.

"Let me guess, you running to those bitches." I stopped, turned around and for a minute, the woman I fell in love with was there. The new Mariah standing in front of me was someone I didn't know.

"Whether you like it or not, they are my family, blood family."

"Well, we know that since they like fucking on each other." Her words were like daggers and I'm not even the one who went through that. My mother loved Mariah to death but if she heard her say that, I'm not sure they'd ever speak again.

"It's better for me to leave." I headed toward my car.

"Which one are you going to fuck, River or Chana? May as well do them both since they're twins." I ran up on her so fast she almost fell backwards. I grabbed her by the hand and led her inside.

"Why you acting like a childish bitch?" I've never wanted to disrespect my wife like that but she had it coming.

"Childish? Bitch? That's what you call your wife."

"My wife would never stoop that low, nor would she say some foul shit to her husband like that. To say I wanted to fuck my own family told me how jealous you really are." River and

Chana were both beautiful women. However, not only were we related, they were taken and so was I.

"Since you wanna be nasty and talk shit, I'm about to humble your ass real quick." She rolled her eyes.

"You wanna know why a nigga stepped out on you all those times." I can't even count how many women I've been with since the two of us were a couple.

"I stepped out because you don't know how to grow the fuck up. You're childish as hell and fucking them, took my mind off of dealing with you." Her feelings were hurt immediately.

"Some of those women had better pussy than you and could fuck me to sleep. I mean one chick, sucked my dick so good she had me calling out her name. Matter of fact, I still have her number." Tears began to fall.

"Each time I laid with those women, it was peaceful. There wasn't anyone bothering me about this bitch or that bitch. One chick in particular begged me to stay as a side chick to you because she fell in love and guess what, my feelings for her were there as well. But you know what?" I was so close to Mariah, I could stick my tongue out and touch her.

"Regardless of how they made me feel in the bedroom, the feelings I caught for the other chick, no one and I mean no one could take my heart from Mariah Winston. Not one of those bitches had me wrapped around their finger the way you did."

"Onyx."

"Nah, let me finish. Since you tryna be tough." I backed away.

"I did ask, Salina to marry me before asking you because we slipped up and I got her pregnant again. She was my first daughters mother so hell no we weren't fucking with condoms." Mariah was taken aback by my revelation.

"You weren't pregnant yet, and I wanted my kids in a two parent household. It would've been easier to leave you then since we had no ties to the other." I laughed.

"The crazy thing was, I didn't even ask because I was in love with her."

"Then why did you ask her?"

"Because even then you were being fucking childish. I didn't wanna live my life trying to raise a grown kid, or with a woman who let me walk all over her. I could've stayed with Salina for all that, which was the plan." In the beginning, Mariah knew about the cheating and come back multiple times. It wasn't until she put her foot down and really left me that I respected her. I stared at her intently and let the next set of words come out with ease.

"I should've never married you." Those words cut her deep. I could tell by the way she gasped and lost her breath.

"I'm gonna have this marriage annulled. You can keep the house, everything in it, and I'll make sure you get all my money."

"What?"

"You're about to have my daughter and I make more than enough off one job to replace what I'm giving you. I'll be by to grab a few things tomorrow."

"Onyx, please don't leave." She yelled at my back.

81

"I gotta go fuck my cousins; remember." I hit her with the peace sign and pulled off.

Damn, it felt good to get all that off my chest. They say holding in secrets can make or break a relationship and it's true. Had Mariah known I felt this way, she probably would've left sooner.

* * *

"Damn, bro. You said all that?" Block sat next to me at the bar. This was the only place to come because at the moment, going to revisit another bitch was at the top of my list.

"She fucked me up by saying that stuff about, River and Chana." Block agreed.

"Arabia said she was acting funny at her house too when she picked her up. It's why she told you to pick Mariah up twenty minutes later." I shook my head listening to her own family say she's changing.

"You really tryna get an annulment already?" I took a sip of my drink.

"With the way I'm feeling right now, yes."

"That's exactly why I'm not getting married. I would knock a bitch head off for disrespecting me like that." Mariah was his cousin and as close as they were, he never took sides. If she was wrong he had no problem telling her.

"Trust me, had it not been, Mariah, I would've broke her jaw." My wife had me so angry, I wanted to hit something. It was the very reason us being separated needed to happen.

"Hey, y'all." Salina sat next to us. I haven't seen her much since she was with that guy. My mother usually brought our daughter to her house and I'll get her from there. That was to avoid any run ins between her and Mariah.

"What up?"

"Laila signed up for recreation basketball. Can you buy her sneakers and she wants a pink ball?" I laughed. My daughter's favorite color was pink and everything she had needed to be in that color or she'd have a fit.

"I'll get them tomorrow."

"I'm out." Block got up to leave. We agreed to meet up tomorrow. Huff was the most wanted man in our area after what he did to Arabia. We were going to hit up some of his spots he always laid low in.

"You ok?"

"I'm fine." Taking a sip, I had the bartender bring me another drink and ordered her one too.

"Onyx, your jaw was twitching and you have those lines on your forehead that show when you're upset." I hated that she knew what my expressions were when I'm mad.

"I'm good. Where's Laila?"

"Your mom has her. Are you sure you're ok?" I forgot she called to say goodnight from my mother's house. The fiasco with Mariah had my mind all over the place.

"What you want?" I wasn't beating around the bush with her. She didn't give a fuck if I had an attitude or not.

"Nothing." She gulped the shot down and got up to leave. I

quickly finished mine, paid for the tab and walked out to find her.

"Salina." She was going in the parking lot. Running to catch up with her, I grabbed her by the elbow and swung her around.

"My bad."

"It's ok. Don't forget, Laila wants pink socks too." We both laughed. As she got in her car, I stood in front of the door to keep her from leaving. I'm not even sure why.

"You want something?"

"Nah." Her hands went to my jeans and as much as this shouldn't happen, I'm about to let it. No one was in the lot and it was pretty dark besides the inside car light.

"Were you ready for me?" She joked about my dick getting hard soon as she pulled it out. I put my hands on top of her Mercedes and let Salina do her thing.

"You better fucking swallow too." I pumped faster in her mouth. Salina ain't never been a slouch with her dick sucking. Hearing her moan made me open my eyes. She had her hands inside her pants playing with her pussy.

A few minutes later, I sent my sperm shooting down her throat. Regret washed over me instantly but there was nothing I could do now. It was done.

"You wanna come over?" Pulling my jeans up, I walked away.

"Onyx. Really?" I turned.

"You got yours too." She yelled out, *"Fuck you"* and pulled off mad. The second I sat down in my car, Mariah was calling me again like she had been doing since I left the house. I sent her a message.

Me: The marriage is over, Mariah. Stop calling me unless you're in labor. I hated to be mean but I was at my wits end with her.

I knew it was the end of us when I allowed Salina to suck me off. No woman could get that close since Mariah and I were married and even two years before when I no longer stepped out.

Now, I wasn't worried about anything. Mariah fucked this marriage up and I'm not gonna feel bad about nothing I do. She did this to us and needed to face the repercussions of her mouth.

CHAPTER 10

Block

"River, you better stop playing." I kept pushing her hands away. We were at the courthouse for her to regain custody of Jasir and she was tryna get a quickie.

"Block, no one is out here. Stop being selfish." I couldn't help but laugh.

"After court we can fuck anywhere you want."

"Fine but I never had my pussy ate on the hood or trunk of a car." I shook my head. River was a freak and I loved the spontaneous ways about her. Getting out the car, I pulled her close to me.

"Why you dressed up as Daria today? What happened to Velma?" River had on a pair of bell bottom looking pants with the chain hanging down. I think they came that way. Her t-shirt was clean but baggy as hell. The sneakers peeked out from under the jeans and her hair was in a ponytail. I'm not to pressed because she had the contacts in.

"First of all, I'm not dressed up as either." She sassed.

"Second, I wanted the judge to see me as who I am and not who they think I should be." She put the crossbody purse on, and stuck her phone in the front pocket.

"Huh? The judge don't care if you buy new stuff."

"Yea but you've gotten me name brand stuff, I can't even pronounce. The judge and social worker would know I didn't buy it." I understood where she was coming from but who cared what they thought.

When she moved into her new spot, Ryan's mother got her a job at the hospital part time. River enjoyed working there because she didn't really have to speak to anyone unless they needed help finding a certain floor. Before she started, she went to a few stores and purchased what I'd consider decent looking clothes.

After the first month of being there, I took her shopping in high end stores. And she was right about not being able to pronounce certain ones. It was funny hearing her trying to say Dolce & Gabbana. Nevertheless, she didn't pick up too much for herself but got Jasir a few things.

In my opinion he didn't need anything else. He probably had more Jordan's, Kobe's and Lebron's than me. His father kept him laced.

Ryan definitely got my respect for being able to hold Jasir down when she couldn't. He didn't try and sleep with her nor did he try and take full custody from River. He was a standup guy and didn't have a hood bone in his body. That's why River got mad at me for snapping after he tried explaining how he didn't know about Chana. Hell, my girl didn't know either but it did bother me that he assumed she cared. That's where my issue was with it. Once she explained it from his point of view, I understood where he was coming from, yet he could've spoke about that another time.

"You worry about the wrong stuff." I took her hand in mine and went up the courthouse stairs. Going through the check in process, I saw this bitch out the corner of my eye. Why was she even here? River must've noticed her too and snatched her hand away. I looked at her.

"Babe, you think she's gonna tell you fucked her for my housing?" River just said anything.

"Get in the elevator." I gently pushed her inside. Once it stopped on the fourth floor we walked off and searched for the room number. Opening the door, it felt like all eyes was on us. This was a mediation case that the judge sat on, but because all the other rooms were in use, they had it in a courtroom setting.

"The fuck y'all looking at?" Dana rolled her eyes and was told to leave if she wasn't family. Her sister was looking down at paperwork and the lawyer I hired for River walked in behind us. When you lose custody of a child it's always better to come equipped with a lawyer.

He had her go up to the desk behind the door. Ryan walked in with Chana and Ernie. They spoke and Chana gave me a hug. She had been by to see River countless times since they met. Ernie stopped by once but when he saw me, he wasn't trying to stick around. I could care less about him having an attitude when I knocked him out.

"Please rise for, Judge Oxton." The bailiff said.

After listening to the judge explain what would take place and how he better not hear outburst and disrespect, the mediation started. River and Ryan both spoke and answered all the questions from the state's lawyer and hers. When it was the social workers turn to ask questions, Clara stepped in front of River. You could clearly tell she had an attitude.

I'm not even sure why she was able to ask anything but the judge allowed it. My lawyer said she'd be allowed if it was in a room. I guess the courtroom setting was throwing me off. In the mediation room, it would've been a long as table with them sitting across from one another so it made sense.

"Hi, Miss Thomas. Do you remember me?" Clara was thirty years old with no kids or a man. She always seemed to be well put together and she wasn't a bother like her sister.

"Yes."

"Good. So, you remember the last time we spoke, Jasir was removed from your custody." Did she really have to ask that?

"Yes." River answered politely but I could tell by her facial expression that Clara was about to aggravate her.

"And why did we remove him from your house before?"

"Your honor, why is this line of questioning necessary?" My lawyer asked.

"I'll allow it in case it coincides with the reason he was hurt again." That made no sense because the shooting was all over the news.

"I went to work and left my son with my mother. When I returned he... he...." River cleared her throat.

"He what?" Clara was pushing too hard and it was pissing me off.

"He was foaming at the mouth."

"And why was that?"

"Your honor." My lawyer tried to intervene but the judge wasn't buying it.

"Answer the question, Miss Thomas." The judge ordered.

"He had taken pills."

"And whose pills were they?" I felt someone sit next to me and saw it was Onyx. I gave him a quick rundown of what was happening since he missed some of it.

"My mother's." River was becoming devastated speaking on the subject.

"Miss Thomas, I wasn't the worker on your specific case but can you explain to the judge why you were taken from your home at a young age?"

"I wasn't taken." River countered.

"Excuse me. Can you explain why child services had to get involved when you were twelve?" Rivers lips began to quiver and her eyes were watering.

"I can't hear you, Miss Thomas." It took a few minutes for her to speak.

"Because my mother stuffed pills down my throat and tried to kill me, ok. She said I was a demon and needed to die." River shouted, shocking the shit out of me and everyone else.

"Then why would you leave your son there with the same

woman who tried to kill you?" River squinter her eyes at Clara before answering.

"Why don't you explain to me why the state made me stay there with her? Why don't you tell the judge how I begged and begged to be removed from my home? How I ran away multiple times and the state continued putting me back in her care because they didn't want to deal with the paperwork. Where was my help, Miss Long, huh? Why didn't the state help me?" River stood up yelling.

"Ayo! That's fucking enough. Bitch, don't ask her shit else." I snapped seeing how much pain River was in. It had become chaotic in there. Clara was asking for me to be removed, Chana was going off and the state's lawyer was trying to have River held in contempt for not answering the question. His dumb ass clearly forgot this was mediation. The judge must've had enough because he told everyone to be quiet.

"We will take a ten minute recess." The judge banged down his gavel.

"Bro, let's go." Onyx had to damn near lift me up to leave. Ryan and Ernie came out the courtroom.

"Don't leave her in there alone." I didn't want Clara to say anything slick to her.

"She's not. Chana won't let anyone fuck with her. Are you ok?" Ernie asked. I guess he was over me hitting him because this was the first time we really spoke. When he stopped by the house to reveal how he was related neither of us said two words to the other.

"Yea, I'm good. She never told me any of that."

"That was hard for all of us to hear but you have to stay calm. The judge will remove you and River needs you for support." Ryan spoke some good shit. I took a walk around the courthouse and returned to find River back on the stand. She wasn't flustered and she blew me a kiss. Once the judge came in, court started up.

"Your honor, Miss Thomas never answered the question about why she left her son alone in the same house her mother allegedly tried to kill her in." River chimed right in.

"Your honor, I apologize for my outburst. The trauma from that incident brought on a lot of emotions." He nodded.

"I was pregnant at a young age and my mother wouldn't let me terminate the pregnancy. I'm glad she didn't because my son is my life." He smiled at her.

"Unfortunately, I had no money for food or diapers and the state wouldn't let me file due to the fact I lived with my mother and she had me on her paperwork. Therefore, I had to get a job in order to at least feed my son."

"Not the question your honor."

"Miss Long, I'll allow it since she's explaining the reason why the situation with her son happened." Clara shut up quick.

"I had been working for two months and my son's father would keep him on his days off. My mother did as well and it was never a problem. I only worked four hours a few days a week and she'd keep him once or twice. I'd have my son changed, left him with snacks, and the television would be on his favorite shows." As she continued, I noticed Ryan tearing up a little.

"Jasir was fine every time I came home except that day."

"So, you chose work over your son is what you're saying?" Clara said making the judge snap his neck to look at her.

"Your honor, my son was two years old at the time. I don't know how he got the pills because they're always in my mother's room, but I found him and the pills in the bathroom." She started to get upset again.

"Seeing my baby dying on that floor almost killed me. My mother even tried to snatch the phone from me so I couldn't call for help. She wanted him to die." She shook her head.

"Do you know that woman." River pointed to Clara.

"That woman wouldn't even let me ride to the hospital to check on my son. She had me arrested immediately without finding out what happened." I had no idea Clara was grimy like that. I wonder how many other moms she did that too.

"I was placed on a psych floor to be evaluated and caught a charge for assaulting a police officer when they arrested me." She turned to face the judge.

"I'm not perfect but one things for sure and that's, that I love my son with everything I have and it's been torture not being with him every day. Lucky for me, his father never left his side." No one said a word.

"One last question." We all sucked our teeth.

"Is it true that the man you're with now, was the reason your son was shot on the playground?" Did that bitch really blame me for the shooting?

"Please don't say anything." Chana begged as she squeezed my hand tight. I looked at her.

"Please. Your outburst can really hurt her case."

"She's right, Block. As hard as it is, stay calm." Onyx said.

"Ok, that's enough. Who Miss Thomas is seeing had absolutely nothing to do with the shooting. Jasir was with his father when it happened and he doesn't have a criminal record or deal with anything illegal."

"I'm afraid he's right, Miss Long. Her relationship does not have anything to do with this case."

"Your honor, I sat here for as long as I can listening to Miss Long tear the defendant down. The only reason she was doing it is because she in fact was having a relationship with the man in question. When he stopped returning her calls and texts, Miss Long's sister made him aware that she was going to take, Miss Thomas son." River looked over at me. I had the messages printed out from Dana in case of emergency and this was it.

"Miss Long, you shouldn't even be on the case." The judge scolded her.

"Miss Long sent messages to, Mr. Winston asking him to come over and she'd make sure, Miss Thomas got her son back. It went as far as Miss Long's sister exchanging sex with the man to give her housing."

"Is this true, Miss Long?" She started stuttering.

"The shooting was random, your honor and Miss Thomas did what she was designated to do by the state. She went to parenting classes for a year, she's been to therapy and even did her hours of community service at one of the daycares." A lot of this information was new to me. Then again, River was very private unless I pulled it out of her.

"Jasir's father has no issues returning custody back to, Miss Thomas. They are friends and co-parent very well. We are asking the court right now to relinquish, Miss Thomas rights for full custody." The judge went over the paperwork my lawyer handed him.

"As long as, Miss Thomas keeps Jasir Rogers away from her mother and anyone else who can cause him harm, I don't see why she can't have custody. I'll have the court clerk type of the paperwork and it should be in the mail within the next few days. Case dismissed and Miss Long, I will be in touch with the state about your behavior." The judge said, banging down that gavel again. River just sat there on the stand crying with her hands covering her face. Chana jumped up and ran over to her. It took River a few moments to get up. Her father and Ryan were next to hug her.

"Congratulations." My lawyer shook her hand. She ran straight to me and jumped in my arms.

"Thank you. Thank you. Thank you. I'm so fucking happy you're in my life. I love you so much, Block." Her tears were falling on my neck. I knew her thanks came from me getting her a lawyer because Miss Long tried her hardest to break her.

"I got you forever and I love you too." She pulled her face from my neck.

"Yes, I said it. I love you too, Velma." She laughed and hugged me tight for the second time.

"Let's go celebrate." Chana said holding her hand up to

show off the engagement ring. Ryan told me about it yesterday when we discussed what could possibly happen in court today.

River said he wanted to speak with me about something and that's what it was. He asked me not to mention it, and they wouldn't either if court didn't go in her favor.

"Oh my God! You're getting married. Can I be in the wedding?" River wiggled out my arms.

"What? Of course. You're my matron of honor and Arabia will be a bridesmaid." Chana's voice trailed off as her and River walked ahead of us.

"Thank you." Ernie shook my hand. It was a long road to get here and I'm happy to have witnessed this part.

"Ok, Bro. Let me find out Cupid struck again for you." Onyx joked as we all stepped on the elevator together. River came to stand in front of me.

"I can never thank you enough for this."

"I didn't do anything. You did by being completely honest and not letting her break you." I pecked her on the lips.

"But she did."

"No, she brought up your trauma knowing you would react but she didn't break you. Your strong, River. Don't let no one tell you different." We walked out the courthouse and River was in shock. Ms. Rogers was there with Jasir in his little wheelchair, my parents, Arabia and Onyx's mother and stepfather. They all had balloons that read *Congratulations*. Deep inside we all knew she would get him back. I'm happy she did because it's no telling what she would've done had it went the other way.

CHAPTER 11

Chana

I was extremely happy for River when the judge granted her sole custody of Jasir. I was more happy hearing Block say he loved her; I think all of us were. She had gone through so much in her life, never feeling love from our mother, not knowing our father, and only having sex with Ryan to teach one another.

Granted, I'm still not comfortable knowing him and my sister was sexually active but who knew.

Ryan spoke with River about being ok with us as a couple, and so did I. Some may say it was a long time ago and that's true, however, me and Ryan would barely touch when we learned the truth. That reassurance of River being ok, made it easier for us to move on.

Last night over dinner when he asked me to marry him, I cried my eyes out. We had just spoke about moving in together and now we're getting married. My father was ecstatic and so was my stepmother, Maribel and my three brothers.

They couldn't wait to meet River and Jasir. None of us ever told them how we were conceived or that my dad was also my uncle. They're too young to understand and we didn't want them judging any of us. All they know was River's mom left me at the hospital, and my dad picked me up. We explained all of that to my sister as well so she knew how far to take the conversation if it came up.

"Are you ok?" I asked River. We were at dinner and the guys stepped out to smoke. Block even invited Ryan and my dad who accepted the invite. The women stayed in.

"I'm worried about Onyx." We glanced at him through the glass window they stood in front of. That man was gorgeous and Mariah was messing up by allowing other chicks to try and stake claim.

"Why?"

"Block told me, he was getting his marriage annulled and already messing with other people."

"Well shit, I would too. His wife is a bitch." I shrugged not caring about calling her out her name the way she did us.

"But she's pregnant."

"And she was pregnant when she came for us. River listen." I turned to her.

"I know you want to see the good in others but a zebra never changes its stripes. There's no way in hell, Mariah just started being a bitch. Whatever happened between them was brewing way before either of us came around."

"Yea, I guess."

"Look at it this way, she one last person invited to the wedding you and Block will have."

"Girl bye. Block said he was never getting married."

"Really? You're ok with that." I've come to learn River wanted to be loved by a man. And I also learned that she dreamed of being married too.

"To be honest, it would be nice to get dressed up for the day but he's right. What happens when the wedding is over and real life kicked back in. Our two cousins are a prime example of what can go wrong in a marriage. Think about it; one day you wake up happily married and the next, your husband moved out and filed to have the marriage annulled." I understood where she was coming from.

"Happiness in a marriage depends on those two people. You can't look at what's going on with them and assume your marriage will be the same."

"True."

"I'm going to go now." Arabia came to the table holding her belly. She was such a sweetheart. I felt bad for how her baby father did her and anyone from the outside looking in, you could tell she was happy he didn't pass.

"Is everything ok?" We asked at the same time.

"Yea. I'm tired." She hugged us before walking outside to speak to the guys.

"Hey, Velma and Aaliyah." Janetta sat down next to us.

"Ugh, ahh. How did she get labeled as Miss Aaliyah and I'm fucking Velma or Daria?" River pouted.

"Y'all fraternal twins, duh! You don't look alike and she damn sure not wearing homeless clothes and aquarium glasses. Never mind the fact you drive around in the Mystery Machine." I couldn't help but laugh. River swung her head in my direction.

"Be happy my son saw past those thick ass nerd glasses and your beady head." I gave her the finger.

"Anyway, I'm here because Arabia making me take her home. Do me a favor, and bring some of the appetizers to my house."

"Nope."

"That's why I'm gonna tell Block to cheat on you." She mushed River and walked away.

"She gets on my damn nerves." River complained but asked the waiter to put an order in for the appetizers she wanted.

"Let's go. I wanna have that celebratory fuck." Block was tipsy so his voice was loud.

"Alright then. I'll see you later." They waited for the take-out, said goodbye to everyone and left. Ms. Rogers took Jasir home an hour ago.

"You ready." Ryan whispered in my ear.

"Yes." By the time we left, our entire party started to head out. Onyx approached me outside.

"Hey, I wanted to apologize for, Mariah."

"You don't have to do that. Besides, it doesn't sound right or even sincere when the person who said it wasn't the one apologizing."

"I respect that. Congratulations, cuz and we have to link up so the rest of the family can meet y'all." We embraced one another. Me and Ryan got in the car and went to my house to celebrate again.

I don't know what him and my sister taught one another as teenagers, but I can say I'm thankful because he was an amazing lover.

* * *

"Maribel, this is, River. River, this is my wife, Maribel and our sons, Jose, Ramone, and Ernie Jr." My father spoke proudly introducing our brothers. They were all under the age of fourteen but old enough to understand we had another sister.

"They don't look alike." Ernie Jr. blurted. He was the oldest and at thirteen, he was tall as heck.

"That's because they're fraternal. How are you older than me and don't know fraternal meant different?" Ramone responded with his sarcasm as usual. He was eleven and very good in middle school basketball.

"Why are your glasses so thick?" Jose asked, taking them off River's eyes and putting them on. He was nine and a pain in the ass.

"Jeesh, it's like looking through the fish tank in these. How can you see anything in them? He joked.

"Jose, apologize right now." Maribel scolded.

"Why? She knows how thick they are, don't you." River removed the glasses out his hand and put them back on.

"You should probably get permanent contacts. Those

Albert Einstein glasses could be used as a Time Machine."
Ramone started cracking jokes.

"At least she's not that ugly when they come off." Ernie Jr.
shrugged walking away.

"Y'all have to be the most ignorant kids I know." My
mother yelled. I've been calling her that since I could remember. She was the only woman in my life as a mother figured.

"It's ok. I'm used to the smart comments."

"That is not ok, honey. Those kids are bad as hell and I keep
telling your father to correct their mouth. But he think it's
funny." We turned to my father who was waving her off to
focus on the news. That man could watch CNN and Fox News
all day, only to try and debate with someone on what's the
truth.

"Anyway, I'm happy to meet you." My mother had both of
us follow her into the kitchen.

"Watch out!" Ramone yelled.

"You would think someone with those glasses saw my ferret
lying there." River jumped and ran around the table.

"It's supposed to be in a cage. Boy get that rat looking
animal out of here." I cursed in Spanish. Maribel was 100%
Hispanic and made sure me and my brothers spoke it fluently.

"Is this all the time?" River questioned the way our brothers
acted.

"All the time and when we go out it gets worse." I
admitted.

"So, River. Your father mentioned you had a son. When do
we get to meet him?"

"The cast on his leg won't be removed for another two weeks. His father said he's too heavy to bring in and out." I laughed. Jasir was tiny like River. Ryan didn't want to aggravate his leg by constantly bringing him places. He did go out for other things like the doctor's appointments, the day River won custody and when they swap but that's it.

"You can visit him at my house if you want."

"I'd like that but I'm telling you now, don't let him come over." River gave me a confused look due to her statement.

"Jasir will come home with a nasty mouth and rude jokes. I'm telling you, your brothers are horrible. I don't know where they get that shit from." We all started laughing.

"Chana, your grandmother wanted me to remind you, orange is her favorite color when choosing a theme for the wedding." Her and my dad have been together for over eighteen years so of course all of her family considered me related to them as well.

"Tell, Abuela, I love her but there will be no orange. I'm not having a pumpkin patch wedding." River thought it was the funniest response ever.

"When are you getting married?" River stopped laughing quickly.

"Never. Me and Block just got together and—"

"And from what your father and Chana told me, you two are in love." River smiled.

"For a man to go off in court the way your father told me, I'd say he won't be letting you go anytime soon. Why not get married?" River shrugged.

"Ma, when you meet him, you'll understand." She put her hands on her hips.

"We know he's a gangsta because he almost knocked your father out over her. In my opinion, he will ask her." She winked at River.

The three of us went out for lunch and it was refreshing just speaking on life, what the future may hold and getting to know one another better. My mom did mention her family wanting to meet River too and she was all for it. The smile on her face made us happy because she never had the family love or anyone she felt loved by, except Jasir. Ms. Rogers and Ryan loved her and in her eyes it was enough. Moving back was the best decision my parents made.

CHAPTER 12

River

Today was going to be a rough one. My father wanted to visit my mother since she left the hospital abruptly after seeing him. I'm not sure it would be a good idea but we'll see how it goes.

It would be the first time I've been at her home considering she had my son taken away. Yes, I left him with her thinking it would be like any other day she babysat but to know she purposely tried to take his life, made me not only angry but despise her.

When she showed up at the hospital, I wondered how she found out; better yet, who told Charlene. Why were either of them there? It never dawned on me that someone had to know about me in order for those two to come. Maybe I'll find out today, maybe not.

"When you get upset, think about how good that dick was to you last night." Block joked, sitting in the car with me. I can't lie though, he had me at his mercy last night. Even with all the experimenting me and Ryan had done in the past, it couldn't compare to the way Block did my body.

"You wanna give me some now. I could use it to relax."

"Hell no. I want you to go in there pissed off. That woman did some fucked up shit to you and my stepson. Whoop her ass if you have to." I smiled at him calling Jasir his stepson. The interaction between those two always make me laugh. They are comical with the jokes while playing his game.

"I can't hit her. She would call the cops on me for sure." He nodded.

"I don't usually hit women but I'll make an exception. Do you want me to do it?" I had to snicker at his statement. For the time that we've known one another, he already showed multiple times that he'd do anything for me and my son.

"No, Babe. If you go to jail, who will I have moaning my name when I do those tricks." He turned his face up.

"You talk a lotta shit for someone who about to get fucked up." I saw other cars pulling up behind us.

"I told you, Block. No one wants me but you."

"And it better stay that way with you too. Ain't no other nigga ever dicking you down." He spoke confidently.

"Not if they can't do it like you." I pecked his lips and rushed to get out.

"Keep playing, River." He yelled over the truck when he got out. I tried to drive my own vehicle but he refused to let my mother see me in it. Talking about let her think you drive a Maserati.

"Hey. You ready?" Mrs. Maribel asked in a concerned manner. She drove over for support. Chana was parked behind them and I saw Onyx and his mother getting out as well. Clearly, everyone wanted to be here.

"Yea. How is my dad?" She pointed to him sitting in the car.

"Nervous." I walked over to him. Opening the car door, he stared straight ahead.

"In order to get closure or other answers, you have to come in." He turned to me.

"Maybe I should try another day. All of you are here and—" I grabbed his hand.

"That's why you should go in. With everyone here, nothing will get out of hand." Block and Onyx were smoking by his truck.

"Well, I'm hoping it won't get out of hand because those two will make a problem for her." I shook my head looking at Block and Onyx.

"Alright." I'm not sure why he didn't want to go in when he was the one who asked me to bring him. Walking next to me, everyone kinda lined up behind us heading to the front door.

"I don't know if she's here and I'm hoping the key was never moved." Bending down to lift the dirty rug, low and behold the extra key was still there. Pushing it in the lock and turning it, Block pushed the door open and went in ahead of me.

"Aye, Louise. You in this bitch?"

"That's one way to find out if she was here." Maribel said,

walking in and looking around. The house was the exact same way as when I left years ago.

The couch was in perfect shape showing no one had sat on it. There was dust everywhere and you could see it because the sunlight beamed inside from the open windows. She never had blinds or shades put up in the house. Me and Jasir were the only ones who had the windows covered.

"She not here." Block said, sitting down on the couch.

"Damn, it's dusty as fuck in here." He waved his hand back and forth.

Moving to where the kitchen was, there was a horrible stench. Walking inside there were the same dirty dishes from when I was here. The small spoon, a bowl that had old milk from Jasir's cereal, and the pan of meatloaf that I soaked for dinner from the previous night years ago, was there too.

Turning around to see if she cleaned the bathroom, I made my way down the hall and looked inside. The pills were on the floor and it made me break down. Memories of that day flooded my mind instantly.

"Come out of there, River." Chana pulled me into the room me and Jasir shared.

"She didn't change a thing."

"No, I didn't." I swung around hearing her voice. Where did she come from? Block said she wasn't here.

"You left this house a mess so until you clean it, it will stay that way." My mother stood there appearing to barely be clinging to life. She was very thin, bags were under her eyes, you could see her chest bones from under the T-shirt and the sweats were filthy. She reeked of cigarette smoke and her hair was matted in different spots. I didn't notice at the hospital but then again with so much going on, how could I.

"You knew I wasn't returning here."

"But you're here now and who are these fucking people. I come out the basement and all these strangers are in my house." That's why Block assumed she wasn't here.

"You really don't remember me?" Chana felt some kind of way.

"Didn't I leave you at the hospital? How the hell would I know what you look like when I'm not even sure I saw you after the delivery." Those words hurt Chana. Her eyes began to water right away.

"Are you sure I'm supposed to be your mother?" The insults continued.

"That's enough, Louise." My mother froze hearing Ernie's voice. Quickly turning around, she stared at him.

"Chana was left behind and I raised her with the help of my wife." Maribel walked around him.

"Hi, I'm Maribel." She extended her hand to shake. My mother rolled her eyes.

"You married him knowing he fucked his sister?"

"Oh shit." Onyx blurted out.

"I'm very aware of the past and yes, I did marry him because we both know, what happened back then wasn't either of your fault." Louise shook her head as she leaned on the wall staring at nothing.

"Every Friday for three months that bitch forced us to drink liquor until we passed out." My mother began recanting the story.

"That was the day my mother went to bingo, and my father fucked other women. Charlene knew that and made us do things that were vile." She shook her head.

"What? How do you remember?" Ernie questioned.

"After the state put her back in the house and you ran away, she made me do those same things to other boys."

"Come again." Ernie was shocked.

"It didn't matter that I was pregnant. She'd invite boys over and make me have sex with them all the way up until I was six months. The only difference was there wasn't any drinking so I remembered everything. Those boys would do the weirdest things to me and she'd allow it because they paid her." Tears cascaded down her face as we listened to what else she endured.

"You left me there to fend for myself; you fucking bastard." She ran up on Ernie and stabbed him in the arm with something. We didn't know until he yelled out. It was a small steak knife. When did she get that?

"I'm sorry, Louise. I couldn't stand seeing you carrying my kids." Chana grabbed a towel from the bathroom. It had a smell to it but Chana needed something to dry his arm off with. It was a superficial wound so there was barely any blood. She still had him run his arm under water to clean it.

"You couldn't see it." The way she scoffed made all of us look.

"Imagine being the one carrying them. The one who had to

push them out. The thought of birthing my brother's kids was disgusting." She started dry heaving for a couple of seconds.

"I begged your mother to leave this bitch there too." She pointed at me.

"Aye! I don't give a fuck who you are, I'll beat your ass." Louise jumped at Block's voice.

"You went out and got a woman beater for a man."

"I don't put my hands on women; only bitches." I stood in front of Block to try and make him relax. Maybe it wasn't a good idea to bring him.

"Why didn't you leave me there? I could've grown up with my father and sister."

"Because that weak bitch of a mother wouldn't let me. That ho over there was left because my mother knew if we waited for her to get better, my father would find us. I didn't know why she had us running when she loved getting the shit beat out of her."

"Yooooo, you bugging the fuck out." Onyx retorted.

"And who the fuck are you?"

"You're great nephew. That's Charlene's daughter; my mother." Louise looked at Mrs. Buggs. Before anyone could react, she smacked the hell outta her. Onyx pushed Louise hard as heck into the wall.

"That was for your mother."

"Louise, what is it that you need to help you get better?" Ernie tried to talk sense into her.

"Now you want to help after you left me. What a damn joke."

"Louise, I tried to find you. When daddy killed her, they said no other person lived with her."

"Your father didn't kill her." A smile appeared on her face.

"I did. I killed both of them and made it appear to be a murder suicide." Was she proud of that?

"What? Why?" I don't know why the question came out. Maybe I wanted to know the truth.

"Because she never disciplined Charlene for what she did us to. Daddy said she did it because she had to give her daughter away. She was upset and took it out on us." She had her legs to her chest.

"I blew his brains out after beating her with a bat. I wanted them to feel what they're precious, Charlene had done to me." Charlene didn't shoot her but pulling a gun on them was close enough.

"That bitch over there lucky, I didn't kill her." She stared straight at me.

"This woman about to make me choke the shit outta her. Call my woman out her name again." Block was mad as hell.

"But you tried to kill my son." She smiled.

"Both of you were an abomination; her too. Any other kids y'all have will be one as well. Your DNA will always be mixed in with your father slash uncle."

"How did you know, Jasir was shot?" She looked up at me.

"That social worker who took him from you came banging on my door. She asked me questions on why was he at the park when a shooting occurred." My eyes went straight to Block. Him nodding let me know he understood that he needed to handle Clara. She had no right coming to this house to say anything.

"Why did you come there?"

"I wanted to see if he died. If he did, then I know you would've killed yourself and I'd be rid of the shame. The disgusting feeling I get every time I see y'all would go away." Onyx had to hold Block back.

"Ok, we're not getting anywhere. Let's go." Maribel said and we all agreed.

"Bye. Nobody asked y'all to come over here anyway. And you're just as nasty being with a man who slept with his sister. Those bitches are demons." Maribel punched her in the face and didn't stop until Onyx pulled her off.

"Chana is my fucking daughter and River will be if she wants to. They don't need your weak ass. Ernie went through the same thing as you minus delivering the kids but he stayed strong and knew his daughters needed him. You." Maribel kicked her on the side.

"You blamed those poor babies and tried to kill my grandson." Maribel kneeled down to where she laid.

"I'm not that bitch you can talk shit to. I'll beat your ass and think nothing of it." Maribel was silent for a moment.

"You need to get help or kill yourself when we leave. The choice will always be yours but fucking with my daughters and grandson, will get you fucked up." Maribel patted the side of her face.

"Let's go. Only a weak woman would allow her past to define her. A strong woman would deal with her demons, continue pushing forward and help other women and girls who have been in the same situation." She came to me once we stepped outside.

"I'm sorry you had to see that and I hope you didn't mind me calling you my daughter and Jasir my grandson."

"I don't mind and thank you for saying those words. I've always wanted to say that to her but didn't have the courage." She put both hands on the side of my face.

"You're stronger than you think. Both of you are." She looked at Chana.

"Louise doesn't blame y'all more than she blamed herself for not being able to defend herself against her sister."

"You think?" She hugged me.

"Grownups always blamed the children even though they have nothing to do with it. That way, they can instill all the anger and hurt on them. Louise can't seek revenge on Charlene because she didn't know where she was."

"Wow. I didn't think of it like that."

"Just from hearing her today and some of the mean things your father told me, Charlene had them doing, I figured it out. It could be more to it but that's the gist of it" The way she worded it did make sense.

All the verbal assaults, disrespect, her making me take pills and trying to kill my son could've been what she wanted to do and say to her sister. Since I was the only one there, I was Charlene. Again, as crazy as it sounded, it made sense.

Taking one last look at the house, I shook my head. The only good memory from here was having my son. She almost took him away from me but God didn't let her. Hoping this would be my last time seeing her, it doesn't change the fact that she was indeed my mother.

Onyx closed she door as his mom sat in the car. Each time she learned something new about Charlene, she'd stare off into space like she was doing now in the car. It had to be hard hearing what her mom did, the same way it was hard to hear my father was my uncle and I had a twin sister.

"I'm gonna have the chef put some food on the grill tomorrow. Feel free to stop by." Block told everyone before they left.

"Are we allowed over?" I questioned getting in his truck. As long as we've been a couple, I've never been to his home. He had always come to me.

"What you mean?" He turned the key, hit drive, and pulled off.

"You haven't taken me to your house. I don't even know if you live in the same town." He let out a chuckle.

"I had to be in love first. I can't have women coming to my place and we just fucking. Then they start showing up when they feel like it and I can't have that." Block was funny as hell.

"Matter of fact, we'll swing by your house to get some clothes and stay at my place."

"Oooohhhh, I get to stay with the infamous, Block at his house?" I made a joke.

"You better hope I let you sleep in the master bedroom since you got jokes." Carefully turning in the seat, I put one of my legs on his side close to the door and managed to sit on his lap facing him. It was uncomfortable but I wasn't complaining.

"That's our bedroom and you better believe I'll be sleeping in that room. The only thing is we won't be sleeping for a while."

"And why is that?" He continued driving with me on his lap.

"Because we have to Christen the bed a few times and knowing my man, it's gonna be a long night." He stopped at the red light.

"As long as you know." We started kissing until horns were going off around us. I hopped back in my seat and placed my hand in his. At this very moment, I was happy and prayed it would stay that way.

CHAPTER 13
Block

"What's up, Lil Man." I lifted Jasir from the back of Ryan's car. His father grabbed the wheelchair while I took him inside.

I honestly didn't think I'd like that nigga, especially since him and River shared a kid. Turned out he was actually a cornball and he loved his son and River, but not in a sexual way. Most baby fathers be on some grimy shit by still sleeping with their kids mother. Once we established that would never happen, I was cool.

"My cast comes off next week. Daddy was going to take me to the store and get a new bike today but he said you were having a BBQ. Why haven't me and mommy been here before?" He was smart as hell for an almost five year old.

"He was and mommy never wanted to come here." I sure did blame her.

"Jerome Winston. Really?" I turned and saw River standing at the top of the stairs wearing an all black maxi dress showing off her shape that I wanted to keep hidden. Her hair was in a ponytail to the side; she had those contacts in and I could see her lip gloss shining from where we stood at the bottom of the steps.

"You need to put on Velma's clothes, Daria's glasses and those beat up converses you don't want to get rid of." River looked beautiful and being selfish, I wanted to keep her beauty all to myself.

"Boy? Be quiet. How's mommy's baby?" She headed down the stairs showcasing the tie up sandals each time she took a step. Once she hit the last step, I smelled her perfume.

"You look pretty, Mommy." He maneuvered into her arms.

"Thank you, Sweetie. And you look very handsome." Jasir had on a pair of Jordan shorts with the shirt and sneakers to match. I paid one of the barbers I'm cool with to go by his house every other week to cut his hair until the cast came off.

"River, you gotta change." I spoke loud enough for her to hear. When she walked away, the dress clung to her ass showing off the roundness of it and I wasn't ok with that.

"Block, stop it. Did I say anything about those gray sweat shorts I asked you not to wear?" I looked at my shorts and nothing was wrong with them.

"Sit here, Jasir while I get you a water bottle for the medication." He was just getting over a cold and the doctor put him on antibiotics. He said they made his throat dry. Following her into the kitchen, I pulled her in the bathroom.

"Where the fuck did you get this outfit?" I closed the door and grabbed the thin material.

"Family Dollar."

"Say what?" I know she didn't just say that.

"Don't judge, Block. They have nice and inexpensive clothes in there." Her arms were folded.

"Ok, I get you're broke but Family Dollar. People only go in there for shit like laundry detergent, potpourri, entertainment stands or coffee tables."

"Babe, it's ok. No one will know I paid $4.98 for this outfit. It was on clearance." She modeled it.

"And they have a clearance section. What the fuck, River. I swear if you break out from that material and a rash forms around your pussy, I'm never fucking you again." She laughed.

"First of all, you always wash clothes when you first purchase them so there won't be any rashes." She wrapped her arms around my neck.

"And second, I specifically wore this for you and you only. Everyone should see Block had a beautiful woman too." I kissed her lips.

"You've been beautiful to me, River. It's the exact reason I told you to let me come over when you got your new place." I placed kisses on her neck.

"Besides those glasses, everything about you turned me on. Your strength, the love you have for your son and how you loved me even though I'm rough." She started to get choked up.

"I don't need a model on my side to show off to family and

friends." I tilted her head back and kissed the tears coming down the side of her face.

"All I ever needed was a woman to be down for me and take care of home. You are her and I'll kill anyone over you and Jasir." She nodded and the two of us started kissing again. She lifted her dress, slid her panties off and soon as I slid in, someone started banging on the door.

"You better squeeze those pussy muscles because I'm not walking out with blue balls."

"Fucking disgusting." I heard Arabia say outside the door.

"I love you, Block."

"Same here, sexy." The two of us got a quickie in, washed up and walked out the bathroom like nothing happened.

"Oh shoot, Jasir's medicine." I told her to go fix her hair and I'd give it to him. Smiling as she walked away, I had to admit to myself that she was the one.

"I'm glad she makes you happy." Arabia was sitting next to Jasir when I handed him the medicine.

"You worried about me being happy when you need to go get your man."

"Auntie Arabia, you have a boyfriend?" I left her sitting there to answer Jasir. Mariah wobbled in with her mom. Onyx hadn't showed up yet and I didn't want no problems. Me and Mariah needed to have a conversation.

"Why wasn't I invited?" She whined soon as I walked over. Grabbing her hand but going slow, we went outside. The chef had his team out there setting up. It was the perfect spot to have a private conversation.

"I'm not about to beat around the bush. What the fuck is wrong with you?" Onyx told me the ignorant stuff she said. He was mad as hell and I don't blame him.

We haven't really seen one another since that happened because I've been supporting River and her family drama.

"Block, I'm dealing with the annulment right now. Can you believe he went through with it?" She shook her head.

"So, you're gonna bypass all the dumb stuff you said to him. How about the fact you're changing on everyone?"

"But I'm not. This pregnancy has been very uncomfortable. Why isn't anyone understanding what I'm going through?" Mariah hated to take accountability.

"You were happy about it in the beginning, what changed." She shrugged with an attitude.

"Why would you say his whole family fucking on each other?" There wasn't any reason she had to say something like that.

"They did. It wasn't a lie." She gave zero fucks about being disrespectful.

"That's why you're in the situation you in."

"Oh, I'm supposed to bite my tongue for those pedophile bitches."

"Aye! Watch your fucking mouth!" She was shocked to hear me snap at her. I have never spoken to her like that before because there was a never a reason to until now.

"Block don't tell me you fell for that homeless chick. She is beneath you and then, you have her son and his father here. The old Block would never deal with someone like that." She sat up to get comfortable.

"I may have messed up big time with Onyx but why are you settling. You can have any woman in the world who had her own money, not on section 8 or already had a kid." Sitting back listening to what she said, had me thinking. Mariah was correct but who was she to say anything about my relationship.

"You're right." Before I could finish, I heard her.

"Oh, she's right, Block. You're settling by being with me?"

"River." I stood and watched Mariah get on her feet.

"I don't need you and never have. You pursued me, remember." She focused on Mariah.

"As far as my son and child's father, that will never be your concern."

"Who the fuck you talking to?" Mariah snapped. Pregnant and all, my cousin was never one to back down.

"You." River removed her earrings, and rolled her hair up in a tighter ponytail where it was no longer hanging.

"Bitch, I'll beat your ass out here." Mariah hooked off on River and before I could react, River started punching my cousin in the face over and over. Snatching River up, I basically threw her in the house to separate them.

"What is going on out here?" My Uncle walked over to Mariah. Everyone else made their way out the door.

"That bitch hit me and Block let her." Why did she lie that fast?

"Hold the fuck up, Mariah. You on some other shit."

Standing out there going back and forth with her and my family, I forgot about River. Moving past them, I saw Ryan taking Jasir to the car. I didn't see her father, stepmother, or brothers here yet. I'm glad because they didn't need to see or hear this. Jasir didn't neither and I hate that Mariah did this.

"Y'all don't have to go." I hated talking like a corny nigga or asking someone to stay where they didn't want to.

"Block, I don't know what's going on between your cousin and the rest of the family, but you know as well as I, that River would never intentionally hit a pregnant woman." I ran my hand over my head listening to Chana.

"We're leaving because it's so much chaos right now, we don't want anyone to say things in the heat of the moment. Certain comments can't be taken back and apologies don't fix everything." I understood where she was coming from and respected it.

"Where's River?" Just as the words left my mouth, she stormed down the stairs with her overnight bag she came with. Chana excused herself.

"River, let me talk to you." She walked around me. I snatched her up and took her in one of the rooms. It bothered me to see the black eye forming and her crying.

"You know, I knew the women you were used to and still gave you a chance. I kept saying to myself, why would a handsome rich man want someone like me? Then I thought, why not, I'm worth it. And as much as I tried not to fall for you, it happened." She turned toward the window.

"This was why I stayed to myself and kept my mouth closed. People like her always look down on the less fortunate."

"River—" She cut me off.

"I haven't been in a fight since the beginning of high school. I can't do this anymore, Block."

"What?" Was she breaking up with me!

"My son was just given back to me and I'm fighting in front of him. I can't have Jasir seeing things like that, especially when I teach him fighting was wrong. Block, you sat there and allowed her to put me down. What kinda man does that to the woman he claimed to love?" Mariah was just venting but it could be perceived that way.

"You didn't let me respond before you came out there." She wiped her eyes and walked toward the door with the duffle on her shoulder.

"She should've never been able to say anything after considering you to settle for me. The conversation went too far and you let it." She shrugged.

"As much as I don't want this to end it has too."

"I'm not tryna hear we over so go home and I'll see you later."

"That's just it, Block. There won't be a later." She turned and walked over to kiss me.

"As long as Mariah stays in your life, and she will because y'all are related, we can never be." Watching her leave had my heart hurting. I was in love with her and this time, I fucked up by not correcting Mariah from gate. She treated Leslie in a similar manner but never put hands on her.

I walked out the room and found my entire family in the living room. Placing my eyes on Mariah, she had the nerve to be crying.

"Get the fuck out!" The room became silent.

"Block, that's your cousin." My pops tried to get me to calm down.

"I don't give a fuck." Making my way to Mariah, I stopped in front of her.

"You put River down for no reason, and then punched her in the face."

"What?"

"Did you expect her not to respond? Huh? Her fucking son was here and her family. What if he saw you laying hands on his mother? Do you even care about anyone besides yourself?" I paced the living room mad as hell.

"That woman has gone through a lot and never once did she disrespect you. You want everyone here to feel sorry because you're pregnant, but did you think about the baby when you hit her first." I stopped pacing.

"If you weren't my cousin, I would've broke your got damn hand for hitting her." I heard someone gasp. I have never spoken to any woman like that in our family.

"Didn't I say get the fuck out?"

"Block." My Uncle Montell pulled me away from her.

"NOW!" Mariah jumped. Her father escorted her out with my aunt following behind.

"Y'all can all go with her and lock my fucking door." Leaving all of them downstairs, I went to my room. As usual,

Mariah caused a lot of unnecessary drama. She would have to be dealt with once the baby arrived.

CHAPTER 14

Mariah

"What has gotten into you? Block and you have been best friends forever. Why did you attack his girlfriend?" My mother bombarded me with questions during the ride home. I went with them to avoid driving, I'm regretting that now.

"She had no business getting in our conversation." My mother turned around to face the back quickly. My father shook his head.

"He loved that woman and her son. Do you know she left him?" I overheard someone asking River why she was leaving but it wasn't my concern.

"That was stupid."

"No woman would stay in a relationship with a man where

she had to fight his family. It can cause friction and others will get involved." I didn't respond.

"He won't say it, but that shit hurt, Block." My dad said as if I cared.

Pulling in my driveway, the car cut off and both of them looked at me. Not feeling an ounce of remorse for what took place, I said goodbye and opened the door.

"You better apologize to that woman for putting your hands on her." My mom said from the front seat.

"That will never happen." I took the key out to open the front door and got out the car. Feeling a presence behind me, I turned to see Onyx making his way toward the house. He parked on the street.

"I'll call you tomorrow." My father started the car as he yelled from the window.

Walking in the house, I jumped when the door slammed. The expression on Onyx's face was unreadable. Placing the keys on the hook, I headed to the downstairs bedroom where I'd been staying since he left. It was hard going up and down every day so the best thing was for me to be on the lower level.

Turning on the bathroom light, I stared at the dried up blood from my nose and the black eye forming. Who knew the bitch could fight? She wouldn't have gotten that many hits if I wasn't pregnant.

"How long are you gonna stare at me?" Removing my clothes to shower while he kept his eyes trained on me, I started the shower. He stepped out which only aggravated me. Did I not turn him on anymore?

Taking a longer shower than expected, I figured he would be gone. Imagine my surprise seeing him handing me the towel. Wrapping it around my body after drying off, I walked into the bedroom.

"The annulment papers haven't been signed; what you waiting for?" I sat on the bed to put lotion on. He used to do that for me.

"I didn't ask for one, you did." I shrugged.

"Do you think it's a fucking game? All this unnecessary drama you causing amongst families. Is it funny to you?" He was seething.

"Onyx."

"Remember that day when you mentioned having to tell me something but my phone rang."

"Yea." I continued putting on lotion and stood to grab some pajamas out the drawer.

"What did you have to tell me?" I wanted to come clean about Sean but he left the house.

"Why does it matter now? You made the choice of not hearing it when you left that night to be with your new family."

"Are you fucking jealous?" He moved in front of me.

"You're jealous over women who just found out that we're blood relatives. Women who damn sure don't want me and vice versa, regardless of the wild things that happened with their parents years ago. And you're jealous of a woman who took your best friend." I hated that he called me out on my shit.

I didn't like that River came in Block's life and he distanced himself from me. He didn't do that when he was with Leslie.

Where did he even run into that bitch at; had they not met we would've never known they were related.

"Then, you put your hands on her for no reason after putting her down to Block, her man."

"Fuck her. Everyone seemed to forget I'm pregnant and she had no business putting hands on me."

"And you had no business putting hands on her. Let me ask you this." He rubbed on his goatee.

"What would you have done if she hit or kicked you in the stomach? Our daughter could've died over your ignorance." He started pacing.

"Tell me what you wanted to that day." Why did he bring that up again?

"It was nothing." I waved him off and put on my nightgown.

"Ok, cool. When were you gonna tell me about the nigga you fucked? I think his name was Sean." Who told him?

"Why would I tell you? Did you tell me all the bitches you fucked?" I smirked because he thought he had me.

"Why would I, when they did?" He shrugged. This mother-fucker always had a comeback.

"They told you when we fucked, right. How I made them cum real hard with body shakes they never felt. Remember, one chick flat out told you she'd fight you over me so tell me again why you thought I needed to verify it." His words were dangerous and he knew it.

"Let's put it all out there, Mariah. We not together no more. You fucked that nigga plenty of times at the hotel. You even called his bitch and did the same thing to her that bitches did to you." How did he know I called Sean's girlfriend?

She kept calling when we were together so when Sean went to the bathroom, I went through his phone and got her number. She was devastated hearing about him stepping out but didn't leave him. When he asked if it were me who did it, I denied it and to this day never told anyone.

"Y'all met at the gym then linked up after; talking about he was training you. Training you to what, fuck him." He was tearing me down right now.

"I don't even blame you because I deserved that shit; I did, But for a woman who didn't want to be cheated on, you went out and did the exact same thing to another woman."

"Onyx."

"That's why when I fucked Sean's girl, I left her with a good impression." *Did he just admit to sleeping with her?*

"Now, let's take it to the present day, right now."

"I don't wanna hear anymore." Heading out the room to get away from him, he followed.

"The night you accused me of wanting to sleep with my cousin, you fucked my head up." I swung around to see him standing there with a disappointing expression.

"Why would my wife say some shit like that to me?"

"I was mad, Onyx."

"Mad." He scoffed up a laugh.

"I was mad too and guess what? I let Salina suck my dick outside the bar that night and I've fucked quite a few bitches since then." My heart shattered when those words left his mouth. He slowly walked to me and place his thumb on my chin.

"Fucking those women did nothing for me because the only woman I wanted to be inside was my wife." I just let the tears fall.

"But how could I be with her when she assumed I wanted my cousins? Why would my wife; the love of my life say something that ignorant to me?" He let go and stared at me.

"My intentions tonight were to go to the BBQ, take my wife home and make love to her if she let me." Walking backwards to the door, he continued talking.

"All you did was prove that getting this marriage annulled was the best option. Goodbye, Mariah."

"Onyx, please don't go. I'll apologize to everyone. Please." He stopped at the door.

"I don't know why I'm behaving this way. You're right, River did take my best friend away but my husband wasn't supposed to leave me too. I love you, Onyx. Please don't do this." I was hysterical at this point. Without saying a word, he walked out and left me there to cry myself to sleep. *What have I done?*

* * *

"Don't say nothing." I snapped at Arabia when she picked me up. We were going to get our hair done at the salon. Well, I was because her new bestie River did her hair at my aunt's house.

"Hello to you too and I'm not saying nothing. I got my

own problems." She pulled off. We rode to the salon in complete silence. When we arrived, both of us went inside only to be greeted by an aggravated Marissa.

"You can't be here today." She spoke with her heavy accent.

"What? I come every two weeks." My due date was approaching and I didn't want my hair a mess in the delivery room.

"Let me tell you something, lady." Marissa came from around the desk she had in a corner.

"I appreciate your business, trust me, I do. But I do not condone you putting hands on my friend." Was she really taking up for River too?

"From the first time you met her; I said she was quiet and doesn't bother anyone. I went back on my camera and watched you be rude to her and even threatened to get her fired." Rolling my eyes, she finished talking.

"That woman don't bother nobody and now she no longer has a man. You are evil." Marissa pointed in her face.

"Look, when can I get my hair done? I'm not trying to hear all this." Just as I said it, River came from the back looking like she been here all day. My cousin was wealthy, why was she still working here.

"You come back on her days off. You go." She tried pushing me out the door.

"It's ok, Marissa. I'm leaving." She removed the apron.

"Hey, Arabia."

"Hey. Are we still on for tomorrow?" Arabia asked about some plans they made.

"Probably not. I'll call you when we can reschedule." River locked eyes with me.

"What? Why?"

"I think it's best to stay away from your family for a while. The jealousy dripping from your cousin is too much and my section 8 ass is beneath all of you. This broke bitch shouldn't even be in your presence right now." The bitch bumped into me on purpose as she walked by. Arabia looked at me.

"I didn't say anything."

"Go sit in the back." Marissa yelled and pointed. I don't care how mad she was; money was power so I know she's happy to do my hair. Marissa better hope I leave a tip.

CHAPTER 15

Onyx

L eaving the house me and my wife once shared the other night, was the hardest thing I ever had to do. Not only did Mariah finally admit to sleeping with the other guy, she pretended as if she didn't care about all the drama she caused.

I've always had eyes on Mariah, so when I learned she dipped out with the dude from the gym, yea it broke me. I could've barged in on them at the hotel but honestly, after what I put her through, it was my karma. Every time they met up, I knew. There wasn't anything my wife could do without me finding out. Crazy how she assumed holding that in meant I'd never hear about it.

The way she went through my phone at night, was the same way I went through hers. The final straw for me was reading text messages telling him how her feelings were involved, and him responding saying he felt the same. That's when I took it upon myself to find out if he had someone.

Lo and behold, Sean had a fiancé at home waiting for him; the same as Mariah. Finding out where he lived, I made it my business to seek her out and sure enough, shorty was down for whatever. The two of us only had a quick rendezvous because she started discussing leaving her man for me and that was never my intention. Mariah wasn't going anywhere, nor was I.

Now, I'm not even claiming her as my wife and sent the annulment papers to her. Of course, Mariah hadn't signed them as of yet and from the way she spoke; never planned to. She forgave me hundreds of times for cheating and in return, I did the same after hearing about Sean. It may not have been with more than him, yet that one nigga experienced my wife and that alone had me sick as fuck.

No one was supposed to know what Mariah felt like, the moans she made, or what facial expressions she made when having an orgasm. However, it was my fuck up so I ate that shit. I've never been a man to seek revenge on a woman for giving me a taste of my own medicine. If I deserved it, then it was what it was.

Pulling up to my mom's house and eerie feeling washed over me and I never had them. It felt as if someone was watching me but who, I'm not beefing with anyone. The people I've taken out during hits have no idea who's done it.

Shaking it off, I opened the door. My mom was sitting on her couch staring into space once again. It's been her normal since everything about Charlene was exposed. Then again,

Louise mentioned more stuff happened after my uncle left. My grandmother was sick and I hated that she was kin to me.

"Hey, ma. What's up?" Stepping into the living room, there sat my grandmother. No one knew what happened to her after the incident at the hospital and no one cared to find out. All I remembered was the techs and nurses lifting her on a stretcher and all of us being told to leave.

"What the fuck you doing here?" She had a devious grin on her face. There was no visible bruises on her body and she didn't appear to have anything wrong with her.

"My daughter owns this house, not you. And by the way, I'm glad you and your wife are over. I couldn't stand her." She responded.

"What goes on with me and my wife was never your business and I know she told you that."

"She did but nothing about her scared me." She removed her legs off the couch.

"Ma, why you allowing this bitch to be here? You know everything she did." My mother was about to answer but Charlene cut her off.

"You believe everything they said, too. Y'all are so gullible." Shaking her head, she reached for the cup on the table.

"Let me tell you my truth."

"Your truth? A'ight. Let me hear it." I gave her the benefit of the doubt.

"Ernie and Louise are my younger siblings." That's one true thing she said.

"Why did you tell my mother you had none?"

"In my eyes they were dead so why would I?" My mother was shocked to hear her say that.

"As far as them being sexually active to one another, that was strictly on them. See, I caught Louise and Ernie one night in the room lying in bed together. They were fully dressed and watching television but why be in the same bed." Was she serious? Siblings did that all the time growing up.

"I never said a thing so when my parents left one night, I asked if they wanted to drink with me. They agreed and got so drunk, the two of them started feeling on each other. One thing led to another and boom, he was on top of her committing incest." She shrugged. The story wasn't even believable.

"You done?"

"Besides the fact they continued sleeping with each other. Once Louise got pregnant, they blamed me as the culprit who forced them to do it."

"Say I believe your story, when did you become attracted to me? You know watching me in the shower, watching me fuck my wife and walking around half naked in my crib tryna get in the shower with me? Had Mariah not stopped you, you would've done it." No one told me about any of that. I had cameras all through my house and saw it with my own eyes.

Being in denial about my grandmother wanting me, I pushed it to the back of my mind and left it alone. Now that everything came out, I believed wholeheartedly what Ernie and Louise accused her of.

"I was coming to ask you a question when you were in the shower."

"You were told to never come upstairs. When me and Mariah were in the pool, you showed up at my house after I told you not to come. And lastly; why you tryna fuck your grandson." She was flabbergasted by how blunt I was.

"It's clear you're not listening." She put her feet inside the flip flops.

"Oh, I heard you but it's clear you had a problem not listening." I got off the seat opposite of her.

"The only reason you're not hanging from a rope is because someone asked me to wait. Otherwise, you would've been gone a long time ago." I was now directly in front of her.

"The fact you're breathing heavy and licking your lips, tells me you are indeed turned on by me and that's disgusting." I grabbed her collar and led her to the door.

"Onyx. You made me nervous that's all."

"Don't bring your ass over here again." I opened the front door.

"Oh yea, no matter where you go from here on out, I'm gonna know. When that ticket gets punched to end your life, I'll be there front and center. Now get the fuck outta here." Tossing her off the porch, she hit the ground. Lifting herself up, blood came out her mouth.

"Onyx." My mother called me. Closing the door, I went to where she sat.

"Please don't kill her." Instead of getting angry, I nodded. Charlene was her mother so I'm sure it's hard to hear. Unfortunately, she'll have to be mad because when the time does come to take her life, I won't have any regrets.

"Ma, I'm going to ask you one time, why did you allow her in here? You know damn well Louise and Ernie weren't lying." She put her head down.

"She was crying at the door about no one loving her. How her family abandoned her and I felt bad." I rubbed her back.

"Regardless of what took place all those years ago, Charlene had a part in it." She agreed, wiping her face.

"I'm just going to lie down." I helped her off the couch and up the stairs. Once she got in bed, she grabbed my hand.

"I want to see, Raymond. Can you bring him here?" Now my mother knew he hated coming to this area. Blowing my breath, I made her no promises but did let her know I'd try. It was all I could do at the moment.

* * *

"Daddy, where is Mariah? She usually picked me up on Fridays." Laila questioned, hopping in the backseat. Most of the time, my wife would get her from my mother's because that's who Laila wanted to pick her up. Lately it was me and that was because she's almost due and didn't need to be driving a lot.

"You know the baby in her belly makes it hard for her to walk." I waited for to put the seatbelt on. Mariah was all stomach but her feet still swelled and her nose had spread like most pregnant women. She was always tired and driving was a task in itself due to how big her belly was.

"I know but you never pick me up from here." She spoke of

her house. To avoid my wife being upset about going to my ex's house, it was best to make my mom's house the drop off spot. Now that we're about to be divorced it didn't matter.

"I'll pick you up from anywhere. You know that." She giggled.

KNOCK! KNOCK! Looking to my left, Salina was trying to get my attention.

"What?" Getting out the car, I had Laila put her earphones on that connected to the iPad. It was no telling what her ignorant mother had to say.

"Can I have some money?" I laughed in her face.

"Salina, you get money once a month from me to keep the bills paid. Anything Laila needed or wanted you know to call and I'll get it. You asking me for extra money never was an option."

"I'm just saying. I've been sucking and fucking you, why not." This was the exact reason, sticking my dick in her mouth and pussy was a mistake. At the time, I didn't think so but now, I know I was wrong.

"Look here." I moved her away from the car. She had a tendency of getting loud and my daughter didn't need to hear it.

"You offered to suck me off on your own at the bar. Me and you having sex, yea I was drunk at the club, you caught me in the parking lot, we fucked in the car and that was it. Stop acting as if I'm coming to see you and laying up with you regularly."

"Well, you'll be laying up with another kid soon because I'm pregnant." Instead of responding, I went ahead and got in my car to leave. That was a hard pill to swallow being it was a possibility the kid could be mine. That night at the club, I didn't recall putting on a condom and now the shit came back to haunt me.

"Tell your precious, Mariah that we'll be sister wives because I'm keeping it." She was getting louder. Looking in the backseat at Laila, she was bopping her head to whatever played on the iPad.

"Get rid of it."

"The only way I'd get rid of it, was if you paid me. And I'm not talking about a few thousand dollars. Nope, I'm talking whatever you get paid for working." Salina didn't know my exact job description but she knew it paid a lot. The bitch logged onto my laptop one day being nosy and I had just got up to use the phone.

My bank info was up and the last deposit showed. The bitch has the nerve to ask me to transfer a million dollars in her account. That wasn't even the full deposit but all she wanted to do was tell people she became a millionaire.

The only person to ever get a dime outta me was Mariah and Laila. Both of them had hefty bank accounts. They'll never want for anything and neither will my new daughter.

"Peace." If she kept the baby and it was mine, then I'll deal with it. Until then, I wasn't about to entertain any of her nonsense.

CHAPTER 16
Arabia

"One more month and it'll be time to deliver." My doctor spoke with happiness in her voice. I still couldn't believe me and Mariah were a month apart for our birthdays and now our kids would be the same. She was due any day now and the family was happy to welcome her daughter.

Unfortunately, her and Block weren't speaking and neither was him and River. He was never one to sweat a woman and he didn't for her either. It was sad because they were in love with each other. I'm upset because we became tight and now she didn't want to hang out. I understood though.

Mariah put all of us in a messed up situation. If River came over and Mariah stopped by, who knew if she would get smart and then we'd be breaking up another fight. It was unfortunate to say the least.

"Thank you." She turned to Deray, who I told about the appointment last minute thinking he wouldn't make it.

"Dad, will you be in the delivery room with, Mommy?" I was hoping he said no.

"Without a doubt." She shook his hand and left us alone. I pulled up the sweats after wiping the gel off and grabbed my stuff to leave.

"Arabia."

"Yea." I had the door opened. Deray had a way of making me succumb to his kisses and there was no way we could have sex in here.

After the last two times, my body yearned for him but I refused to give in. I even changed the password on my security camera so when I did masturbate, he couldn't watch. Deray loved watching me do myself and I enjoyed him do it as well.

"How much longer are you gonna make me suffer?" He placed one of his hands on my back and moved me close.

"I'm not making you suffer, Deray. I have to figure out if you're worth me taking another chance on." Pushing myself away, hurt washed over his face.

"The pain and agony I went through thinking you were dead, was bad. I could've lost the baby had my family not been there to support me. Then what, I wouldn't have had anything remotely close to remember you by." He didn't say a word.

"I wanted to die, Deray just to be with you again. What if I killed myself thinking you were dead?" Again, complete silence.

"If you watched the camera, then you know how miserable I was. My eyes were swollen from crying so much. I wasn't eating, sleeping and barely left the house. What part of you hurt me don't you get?"

"Arabia, I'm sorry. I fucked up bad." He wiped my eyes. I hated that this baby could make me cry at the drop of a dime.

"I'll never do that to you again. I mean, hopefully it won't ever come to that." He made me crack a smile.

"Can I come sit with you then? It's getting close to the delivery date and I'm not comfortable with you being alone."

"Why not? I have a big house. You can sleep in one of the guest bedrooms." He sucked his teeth.

"Take it or leave it."

"I'll be there later on tonight. I have to pack some clothes." He walked me to the car and both of us went our separate ways. I hope having Deray stay doesn't make him think we'll have sex because as horny I've been, that would complicate things.

* * *

"SURPRISE!" I turned to see my whole family. Deray asked me to attend a party with him and we only had to stay an hour. He didn't say it was for me.

"What's going on?" No one moved and I didn't know why until my mother turned me around. Deray was on his knee with a velvet box holding a huge diamond ring.

"I messed up, Arabia and I'm so fucking sorry. You mean everything to me and Amani. Will you marry me?" I could barely see him because the tears were coming down extremely fast. Everything was blurry at the moment. At the doctor's appointment I told him time was needed, now here he was on his knee proposing.

"Hurry up and answer him. Shit, I'm hungry." As usual, my mother had to say something smart.

"Yes. I'll marry you." He placed the ring on my finger, stood and kissed me passionately.

"Thanks for not embarrassing me." He whispered and kissed my neck. Deray had a hold on me whether he knew it or not.

"If this was when you first returned, I would've." He pecked my lips and held my hand to go sit.

"What in the world?" Once I was able to get a full view of the hall, there were baby gifts everywhere. I looked at Deray.

"Me and your brother had a conversation. He gave me this spot to rent out and I handled the rest. You didn't have a baby shower date set so I made it happen."

"Yea, but how did you get the family here? No one knew you." Deray was never a secret, I just didn't tell anyone because Huff was supposed to be my man at the time.

Glancing around the room, my entire family was there; including Mariah who appeared to have had an attitude. Today wasn't the day for me to be aggravated so I avoided her and went to the other side where the big chair was at one of the tables.

"Congratulations, Arabia." Her voice made me want to smack the hell out of her. His mother had joy in her voice and it irked me.

"It's your day, Arabia. If you want them to leave, I'll make them go." Deray spoke of his parents, Tricia, her girlfriend, Amani and some other guys.

"You're right, it's my day. Just tell them to stay away from me." He helped me in the chair and had them go sit elsewhere.

"It's not fair to speak to him and not his family. They're not the ones who faked his death." Block sat next to me and Onyx on the other side digging in the vegetable tray.

"No, but they went along with it. At least Deray wasn't feeding me lies."

"Do you hear yourself? He told them not to tell you. That lie came from him, duh!" Block went back at me.

"Whatever. Why you bothering me? Where's River?"

"Who the fuck cares?" He removed himself from next to me. Me and Onyx looked at each other.

"He miss her." We both said at the same time and started laughing.

Throughout the evening, my family and others congratulated me on the baby and engagement. We received so much stuff, Deray was taking some to his house for now. We hadn't decided whose house we would live in so as of right now, the baby will be at mine.

"Auntie Arabia." I heard and there was Jasir walking slowly toward me. Block must've saw him because he ran over and scooped Jasir up. He had the cast removed and had to take his time moving around.

"I'm sorry, we're late. I had to close the salon and then go home to change. Chana didn't want to bring him alone. Anyway, here you go." She handed me a card.

"It's not much but there was no time to get a gift."

"Hi, I'm Deray." River looked at me and then, Deray.

"Wow! You're really alive." He laughed and shook her hand. She introduced him to Jasir and Chana, who already had a plate in her hand. When did she get that?

"Is the party over?" Jasir questioned when Block sat him next to me.

"Not yet. We just took all the gifts to the car, that way we don't have to do it when it's time to go."

"Oh. What did you get, Auntie Arabia?" He always made me smile. Out the corner of my eye, Mariah was slowly making her way over.

"Well, well, well. Isn't this one big happy family." River rolled her eyes. Where was Block and Onyx? Nobody wanted to deal with her shit.

"Mariah, don't start." My mother walked up with a drink in her hand.

"If you wanna fight, wait til you have that baby. I don't want to see you get two pieced again." Janetta made a joke.

"Ain't nobody two piece shit."

"The hell if River didn't. She was like, Pow, Pow, Bam." The sound effects and her demonstrating had me laughing. Mariah was mad as hell. I wasn't present for the fight but Block said, River was giving Mariah the business too.

"It's probably best if we go." River went to grab Jasir.

"Mommy, can we get some cake first?" She told him yes. Her and Chana headed to the food table where it was.

"Ma, why you starting?" I asked.

148

"Mariah needed to learn how to keep her mouth shut. She has it out for River and it don't make no sense." I had to stare at my mom for a minute. Was she becoming soft for River?

"I'm about to be out." Block made his announcement at our table. He wasn't loud though. He gave me a hug.

"Go talk to her." I spoke softly.

"She doesn't wanna be around if Mariah is. Ain't shit I can do about that when we're related." He shrugged, kissed my cheek, and headed towards the door.

"He know that girl want him." My mother spoke sitting next to me. Mariah was on the other side snarling at everyone.

"Babe, I'm ready." I told Deray. The party was pretty much over anyway and it was getting late. We arrived at three and it was after eight. That was long enough for me. We had eaten dinner, took photos, played games, opened the gifts, cut the cake, and danced. It was a perfect day.

Deray's parents did approach me and apologized. She tried to get me to understand her logic but nothing they said, could get me to forget what they did. I understood why Deray felt the need to play dead but damn, his entire family was in on it. They could've at least told me on the side even if we weren't able to be in the same place. I wouldn't have been so miserable.

One day, I'll get over it. It took some time to speak with Deray and he was calling and trying to see me nonstop.

None of them even called to check on me when he supposedly died but once or twice. Granted they attended the doctor's appointment but I know why now. Deray wanted to be there on facetime but after that, I hadn't heard from his family until his mother's phone dialed me by accident. And that's where my problem was too. I was pregnant with Deray's child and the family turned their back on me.

They didn't have to beg me to speak but a simple apology wasn't sincere enough for me either. Especially, when we were very cool before the fake death.

"Now that tonight's over, can I make love to my fiancé." Deray whispered, helping me out the chair.

"You have to find out at the house." I smiled. We intertwined our hand and walked out to his truck. The party planner said she didn't need any help because her team was there to help clean.

Saying goodbye to everyone, Deray assisted me in the truck. It took him a few minutes to get in. I noticed him speaking with the guys who he knew. Once he sat down, aggravation was on his face.

"What's wrong?" He put the key in the ignition.

"I'm taking you to my new house." Oh, he was full of surprises.

"What?"

"We'll discuss that later. Look." Backing out the parking lot, I noticed another car following. Assuming it was his friends, I thought nothing of it.

"Arabia."

"Yea." The same car was still behind us.

"Your ex was spotted two blocks away with two car loads full of niggas." Huff was really getting on my nerves.

"What?" Panic kicked it right away.

"Relax. My boys are aware." That put me at ease a little.

"What the hell?" I shouted, hearing a loud noise on side of his truck.

"Fuck! They're shooting." Looking out the side mirror there was a black car with a dude hanging out.

"Get down, Arabia!" Was the last thing he said before hearing constant gunfire. Please let me and my baby make it out of here. I couldn't believe Huff was really trying to kill him.

CHAPTER 17

River

"Why didn't you talk to him?" Chana asked, strapping Jasir in the back seat. We were in her Kia Sorrento. It was nice as hell and put my van to shame. As much as I would love to get a new car, my finances aren't enough for me to afford a car note.

"He saw me, Chana. He could've spoken to me." She hopped in the front seat.

"Why would he speak to someone who told him she couldn't be around him if his cousin was there?" She made sense but still, he didn't say hi or anything.

"He looked so damn good." I smiled as she pulled out the lot where the baby shower was held. Block had on a pair of jeans, Jordan's as usual and a T-shirt. There was nothing fancy about his attire but then again, he turned me on no matter what he wore.

"What's going on there?" She stopped short. The street was

blocked off by cars and trucks. People were running but we couldn't see why.

"Oh wow. It looks like a bunch of cars shooting at each other. Let me get the heck out of here. We do not need to get caught up in that." As she drove to get us home, Block was on my mind heavy. Going through my phone, I went into the photos.

"Chanaaaaaa." I sang closing out the app.

"What?" She took turns looking at me and then the road.

"Do you mind keeping, Jasir?" Ryan had to work which was why he wasn't here. Block's family was cool with him and now that we were related to Onyx, we kinda meshed the family ourselves.

"For?"

"I have to get my man back." She smiled.

"You want me to drop you off?" I thought about it and decided not to make her go out the way. Block lived forty minutes away from me.

"No, I'll take my van." Once we got to the house, I ran in to grab an overnight bag for me and Jasir. She waited with him in the truck.

I kissed him goodnight, gave her a hug and hopped in my van. Not wanting to hear him tell me no, I went to Block's house without so much as a text to let him know I'm coming. He doesn't allow women there so I wasn't worried about that.

Parking at his house, I saw his truck was there as well as a brand new corvette looking car. The temp tags were still on and the dark blue was beautiful. Unlocking the door with the key he gave me, I heard music coming from the sound system. Running up the stairs to change into nothing, I caught him coming out the bathroom with a towel wrapped around his waist.

"What's up?" Cracking a smile because he didn't ask why I was there, I removed my clothes and stood there naked.

Not wasting any time, Block lifted me on the dresser and spread my legs wide. His hands roamed the top of my legs and one found its way in between. Sticking his finger in my mouth with his free hand, I slowly guided it down my chest, onto my stomach and placed it inside my love nest.

"Sssss." My head went back when he took over.

"Don't stop. Yessss." Just that fast, I encountered my first orgasm. It felt so good, my body shook for a few seconds.

"Now, tell me why you here." Lifting my head, my eyes met his and all the love he had for me showed.

"I missed you." Helping me off the dresser with one hand, he let the towel drop and in a swift motion, made us one.

"Shit, River. You wet as fuck." I had him lie back on the bed, stood on my feet and rode the heck out of him. I made sure to drop harder, to feel his dick deeper. Not sure why I did that when he was busting me wide open.

"Fuck, Block." He sat up and pulled me in for a kiss. Our pelvises were in sync as we continued fucking the hell out of one another.

"Don't leave me again." He squeezed my ass and moved my lower half in circles.

"I won't." He flipped me over, opened my legs wide as they could go and had me begging for mercy.

"Ain't nobody ever feeling inside this pussy, River. We clear on that!"

"Yessss. Oh gawdddd. Yesss." His finger was plucking my clit gently, driving me insane.

"Make that pussy squirt for me." Pulling out and ramming himself in had my eyes rolling. I couldn't move or do what he asked. The euphoric feeling had me on cloud nine. When he let my legs go, and substituted his dick for his mouth, my body shook uncontrollably. I have never in my life felt anything like this.

"Ain't no man gonna do your body like this." He kissed my stomach, turned me over to get on my knees, stuck his dick inside my pussy and once that one finger went in my ass, that was it. Block had total control over me and he knew. That man could ask me for an orgy right now and I'd say yes.

"Fuck! Got dammit, Block." I was pounding on his bed while he continued fucking both of my holes with his dick and finger.

SMACK! His free hand went to my clit and another orgasm overtook my body. He removed his finger out my ass, spread my cheeks wide and fucked me even harder. He was teaching me a lesson and I was here for it.

"Get the fuck up." My body was weak as hell. Moving me off the bed, he bent me over to touch my toes, bent his knees too dig deeper and my whole body collapsed from the orgasm. He didn't stop and got on the floor with me. Turning me back over, he placed one leg on his shoulder and pushed himself in. Our tongues met and we were once again in sync.

"I'm about to cum." Moving faster inside me, my nails dug into his back making him yelp like a wounded animal.

"That's right, River. Fuck me back." Sliding my hands under my ass to give me a boost, I pumped from the bottom and shortly after, Block released everything he had. We both laid there breathing heavy.

"That was intense as fuck." He whispered with his arm over his face.

"I'm sorry."

"River, I can't control what Mariah says or does but I will always make it my business to make sure she doesn't overstep."

"Why did you let her say you settled with me?" I was becoming upset laying there.

"I was gonna say, you're right she wasn't like any woman I've ever met, but she was mine and ain't no changing that." Rolling onto his body, he held me tight.

"I told you, your broke ass had me stuck. I'm not a fake nigga and if you had let me finish speaking, you would've heard me correct Mariah." Block was right. He never got the chance to respond due to me barging in on the conversation.

"I'm not gonna hurt you, River." His hands were on my back.

"I won't hurt you either but I don't want you battling with your family over me." He made me stare in his eyes.

"I'll battle anyone over you." Kissing his juicy lips got us aroused and we were back at it. This time we had sex in the shower and the bathroom floor. When it was time to sleep, we passed out; at least I know I did.

* * *

"What?" Block shouted, waking me out my sleep. It felt like I just closed my eyes. Sitting up to wait for him to get off the phone, I rubbed his back.

"I'm on the way." He disconnected the call.

"You ok?" Hopping out the bed, he rushed to get dressed.

"Someone ambushed Deray and Arabia when they left the baby shower."

"Oh my God!" Jumping out the bed, I threw on some sweats and a shirt that I had over here. He passed me a pair of Air Max he purchased me. He never removed any of my stuff from his house.

"We have to get to the hospital." We got in the truck and I had to hold on to the door handle due to how fast he was going. Once we got there, Block grabbed my hand and we basically ran in. His parents were there and so was Mariah, Onyx and more family walked in behind us.

"Well, well, well." The voice made me cringe. What was he doing here? He was texting me nonstop for the last two months threatening to tell my man about us. Ignoring him in hopes he would go away, he had a smirk on his face. Please don't let him announce what we've done.

"Just the nigga we been looking for?" Onyx had his gun on Brandon but why. Did they know one another?

"Fuck y'all."

"What nigga?" Block let go of my hand and walked straight toward him until Brandon pulled a gun out.

"Y'all turned on me for that nigga, who was supposed to be dead."

"Turned on you? Nigga we didn't even know about him. We stopped fucking with you for putting hands on my sister." Block said making me very confused.

"Then, y'all killed my parents." He sounded like he was about to cry.

"You can't be mad at the repercussions when you're the one causing it." Block was right. People always wanted you to take it easy on them no matter how bad the situation was that they caused.

"Whatever." He focused his attention on me.

"If that's the only reason, then why you fucking my bitch. Block, we ain't never slept with the same woman." You could hear a pin drop when he said that. All eyes were on me.

"You fucking my sister's ex?" The hate on his face made me upset. His sisters ex name was Huff. How did he figure we were sleeping with the same guy? Unless, Huff was... oh my God!

"Block, can we speak in private?"

"Nah, tell him, River how me and you hooked up twice a week. That's my top bitch and she gets paid very well for what we do behind closed doors. Ain't that right, River. That pussy A1 too ain't it, Block." Was he making a joke out of it?

"Oh, that bitch a ho." Mariah said and before I could hit her, Onyx stopped me. She was talking shit but knew not to move from behind him. Pregnant or not I was ready to knock her fucking head off. I walked over to Block.

"Babe. Please let me talk to you." He snatched away when I grabbed his hand.

"Get the fuck out!" His tone was loud and everyone was staring.

"Please. It's not what he's saying." Block looked up at me.

"Did you fuck him?"

"Will you let me explain?" He wasn't hearing anything I had to say.

"All I need to know is, did he pay you to fuck?" My head went down in shame. There was no getting through to him so I stopped trying and accepted defeat.

"Where's Arabia? Did they say if she was ok?" He left me standing there.

"Fuck that bitch, Block. River for everybody. Let's finish what we started." I couldn't believe he was in the hospital with a gun challenging Block to a fight. His father pulled him outside.

"I'm a bitch, Brandon." I walked towards him pretending the gun didn't bother me but he wasn't about to disrespect me.

"Brandon?" I heard someone sound as confused as me when they called him, Huff.

"You wasn't saying that when your ass was moaning, were you." He focused back on me. They all knew we had sex, wasn't no use in trying to hide it.

"The only reason you're really mad is because I wouldn't let you and that nigga run a train on me." I stood directly in front of him.

"You beat my ass that night too. Now you're mad I'm with someone else." How dare him even bring up what we did when he was sleeping with various women?

"Nobody cares about you and him. I know his money long so he paying you better than me." I slapped fire from his ass.

"Bitch."

POW! My body collapsed when the bullet hit me.

"FREEZE!" Was all I heard before feeling myself choking on my own blood.

CHAPTER 18

Mariah

Finally, someone put that bitch out of her misery. How do you come to a hospital with a man and your pimp, called you out? Arabia wasn't gonna be happy hearing her new bestie was sleeping with her man at the time.

River must've been a low budget ho because she damn sure didn't come up off whatever money he gave her. The bitch was still broke as fuck.

"I'm not going to jail." Huff shouted, and continued firing off shots.

The cops were trying to get him but he ran through the hospital doors. All of sudden there was a lock down being put in place. People were hiding, nurses and doctors didn't know what to do and that stupid bitch was gargling on her blood. I'm not saying I wish death on her, but she ran her mouth and got what she got.

"Shit. Stay here." Onyx said. He had pushed me in the bathroom that was next to the nurses station where we were standing before the shooting took place.

"Onyx—" I stepped out to regain his attention.

"Not right now, Mariah. My cousin was shot and—" He stopped when he noticed my pants were wet.

"What the fuck? This can't be happening." I was a week overdue so it was definitely happening.

"Yo, this woman's water just broke." Did he just make it seem as if we weren't together? He rushed to the nurses desk and pulled one of the ground.

"We need a wheelchair. Ma'am did you have any contractions yet?" I shook my head no. Someone brought a chair and Onyx helped me sit.

"Ahhhh!" I screamed when a pain shot through my body. It felt like someone had a knife inside my stomach and was dragging it across the lining.

"Ok. I'm going to assume that was a contraction. We're going to start counting how far apart they are now." I took breaths in and out to keep me from panicking. That did not help one bit. When the next one came, the pain was even more intense. My stomach was hard and I could feel more liquid seeping down my leg.

"We have to deliver in one of the rooms since the hospital was locked down." A doctor said, closing the door. At least there was a curtain as well and I has some sort of privacy.

"We have everything down here for emergencies so you and the baby will be fine." Glancing around the tight room, Onyx was nowhere to be found. Where did he go?

As the nurses scrambled around in the room to prepare me for birth, Onyx stepped back in. He had a devastated look on his face. Not caring what happened out there, I reached my hand out for him to come closer. He can be mad all he wanted but this baby was coming and he was going to be here for support.

Two hours later, our daughter Heaven Lucille Buggs was born at seven pounds, six ounces. Onyx smiled after she came out and was the first person to hold her. Once the doctor left, the nurse helped clean me up by having the tech move me into a wheelchair to go in the bathroom. The lockdown was lifted an hour into my delivery but it was too late for me to move upstairs.

"Onyx, I'm sorry about everything between us." I managed to get out. I was exhausted and wanted to sleep but my conscience wouldn't allow me to until he knew my feelings.

"Having my daughter is the only thing I'm worried about right now." Respecting his answer, I slowly rolled over, pulled the covers up and went to sleep. I'm not about to argue with him right now.

* * *

"Wake up, Bitch." A male voice spoke in my ear. Slowly opening my eyes, some man stood there I've never seen before. The hospital room was different too. They must've brought me up when I was asleep.

"Who the hell are you?" He was handsome, dressed nice and resembled someone I knew.

"Where the fuck is my brother?"

"Your brother? I don't even know who you are; how would I know where your brother was?" He laughed as I sat up.

"You were the last one seen with, Sean. Where the fuck is he?" My mouth fell open hearing Sean was missing and even more, seeing his brother in my hospital room.

"How do you even know me and what are you doing in my room?" Obviously, Onyx wasn't here because this would not be happening.

"Your friend told me."

"I don't have any friends so whoever told you anything, lied." I'm not admitting to nothing. Especially, when this man could be unstable.

"Bitch, where the fuck is my brother?" Gripping my hair tight, I felt this situation was about to get out of hand. Pressing the nurses button, I waited for someone to answer. Just my luck, it kept making the noise to call the nurse station, yet no one answered. Where the hell were they?

"I'm not gonna ask you again." He gripped it tighter making my eyes go into slits where I could barely see.

"I don't know. The last time we saw one another, we broke it off. Feelings were involved so we stopped seeing each other." I cried out.

"You're lying."

"I swear. I haven't seen or heard from Sean in months." I was trying my hardest to pry his hands from my hair.

"Now, Mariah. Why you lying about being with that man's brother?" Salina stepped in with a smirk on her face. I should've known her trifling ass was behind this. But who told her about Sean?

"You know damn well, I been with Onyx." The guy let go and slammed my head against the bed.

"Speaking of him, where is he? Y'all just had a baby and he's not here." She put her index finger under her chin.

"Oh wait. He probably at my house waiting for me to ride that dick again." That was always her get back at me. I blame Onyx for backtracking. The least he could've done was search elsewhere for pussy.

"Really?" The guy was aggravated.

"Can I help you?" Now the nurse wanted to get on the intercom.

"Please call the cops and have them come to my room for unwanted guests." Outta nowhere the man backslapped the shit out of me. Trying to get off the bed, I fell and hit my head on the heater by the wall. He kneeled down next to me.

"If I find out you had anything to do with my brother's disappearance, I'm gonna kill you." He banged my head on the heater twice before walking out.

"Tsk. Tsk. Tsk. Trying to get one over on, Onyx was your downfall."

"What?" I rubbed the back of my head and felt something wet. Pulling my hand away, it showed blood.

"You and I both know he found out and took that man's

life. When his brother finds out, you're gonna be on his most wanted list."

"What you mean Onyx did something to him?" She laughed.

"You really are dumb. Even I know when we were together he had eyes on me at all times. I couldn't take a piss without him knowing about it." She backed up as I put my hands on the bed to help me stand. I saw the specks of blood on the sheet that must've rubbed off my hand when I felt my head.

"Onyx knew when you stepped out the first time even though he may not have said it. Depending on how many times you did it, trust and believe he knew about each rendezvous." Was she right? Did Onyx know more than he led on?

"Anyway, I'm only here to let you know me and Onyx fucked." I laid in the bed on my side.

"He told me, Salina." She got off on relaying bad news to me.

"I guess he mentioned our new bundle of joy coming in nine months." She rubbed her stomach to be funny.

"Onyx would never fuck you without a condom." She threw her head back and cackled. That's when I remembered him saying, he'd never use a condom with his baby mama.

"Whether you want to admit it or not, his dick was addicted to this pussy. Hence the reason we kept fucking while you two were together." Her words were cutting me deep as hell. I refused to let her know and let her finish speaking.

"My question to you is, who is the father to that baby you just had? If my calculations were correct, you and Sean stopped soon as you told Onyx you were pregnant." This bitch knew too much information. Where was she getting it from? Before I was able to kick her out, Onyx stepped in.

"Are you gonna answer her, Mariah because I wanna know too." Was he here the whole time?

Fuck my life!

To be Continued...

Coming Soon

All I Want Is Forever

Now Available on Amaozn

I Gave My Heart
To A Jersey Killa

Sincerely Yours:
Kamali & Alori

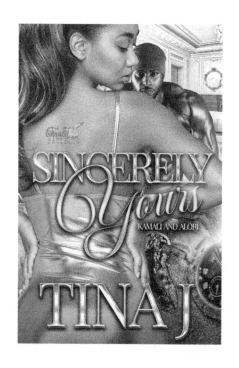

Made in the USA
Monee, IL
06 October 2024

67281711R00108